## "I'm glad you're safe."
## That, at least, was true

"You don't think I'd let anything happen to me now that I've got you, do you?" Cole said.

Lindsey closed her eyes. There was no way she could ever subject herself to such agony again. Explaining to Cole wasn't going to be easy.

He reached for her, dipping his head to possess her lips. Here was no gentle kiss of friendship. This was the kiss of the conquering hero, a man who had faced death and won.

She drew back, and a rough thumb caressed her throbbing lips. "It was worth a little fear for a welcome like this. I want to know that this kind of homecoming is always waiting for me. Marry me."

The casualness of his words was belied by the intent look in his eyes as he made to pull her back into his arms....

**Jeanne Allan**, born and raised in Nebraska, lived there until she married a United States Air Force lieutenant. More than a dozen moves have taken them to Germany and ten different states. When not moving, she is a seasoned volunteer, does all kinds of crafts, makes stained glass windows and, with their two teenage children, enjoys nature walks, bird-watching and photography at their cabin in the Colorado mountains. She has always liked to write, but says her husband bullied her into writing her first romance novel.

## Books by Jeanne Allan

HARLEQUIN ROMANCE
2665—PETER'S SISTER

# *When Love Flies By*

## Jeanne Allan

# *Harlequin Books*

TORONTO • NEW YORK • LONDON
AMSTERDAM • PARIS • SYDNEY • HAMBURG
STOCKHOLM • ATHENS • TOKYO • MILAN

Original hardcover edition published in 1986
by Mills & Boon Limited

ISBN 0-373-02845-8

Harlequin Romance first edition July 1987

# CHAPTER ONE

THE day was hot, the sun shining down with blazing intensity, the sky painfully blue. Adults complained to each other in low murmurs about the stifling heat and fanned themselves with their programmes as they waited for the show to begin. The women were wearing large hats to shade themselves from the fierce rays. Lindsey's mother's hat was pale yellow, and it dipped low in front, hiding eyes which sparkled with excitement. Ignoring the heat, the children played tag and raced about in sheer exuberance, their high spirits an exaggerated expression of the low-keyed anticipation displayed by the adults. A temporary dustbin was a 'safe' place, and Lindsey stood barely touching it, breathing deeply from her mad dash to safety. Flies buzzed lazily over the bin, settling now and then on half-eaten hamburgers, only to erupt in a cloud when another child dashed by. A foetid odour of food too long in the sun sent her running for a more pleasant refuge, but before she had gone far, a drone in her ears rose in volume to a loud roar, and she raised her eyes expectantly.

Emitting a piercing whine, a small jet split the skies above her. With nonchalant ease, the plane flipped on to its back and screamed the length of the runway, seemingly only feet above the concrete. Another flip and the plane righted itself before ascending into the shimmering blue sky. Before the crowd could breathe a shaky sigh of relief, two more jets flashed by, their wing tips flirting with each other and disaster. The awed silence of the crowd was a testimony to the skill and

5

courage of the pilots, and a low murmur of appreciation greeted their passing. More planes followed, each seeming to surpass the previous in feats of skill and daring.

Impatiently Lindsey hopped up and down on one foot. These preliminary demonstrations held no interest for her, not today. Because today, her father was scheduled to fly. Not one of these planes screaming by now, but a newer, faster model. She had seen him earlier in his green flight uniform when he'd made her promise to wave at him as he flew over. She didn't completely understand it, but she knew that whenever her mom pointed to a plane and said that her daddy was flying it, Lindsey's chest seemed to swell until she thought she would burst with pride. He was special, her father. She knew her mom thought so, too, because her eyes would kind of light up when she watched him fly. Her mother would giggle like a little girl, and sometimes even give a little hop of excitement. Then, when Lindsey's father was back on the ground, her mother would run over to him, her eyes shining and he would swing her off the ground. Later, he would toss Lindsey up on his shoulders, and she would tell him how excited the two of them had been, and her father would laugh and grab her mother's hand, and the three of them would head for home.

That was the way it was supposed to happen. Laughter and fun and excitement. Not a crowd stunned into silence. Not that horrible scream tearing from her mother's throat, a scream that echoed around and around in Lindsey's head. She could see the other women, shock on their faces, holding back Lindsey's mother when she tried to race towards the end of the runway—the end of the runway where a bright flash of orange had preceded an ominous black mushroom. The dull boom had reached their ears later. Scared by the wailing from

Lindsey's mother, and uncertain of what had happened, small children began to cry, only to be harshly hushed by their mothers. Tall men in blue gathered around Lindsey's mom and led her away. It was a few minutes before anyone remembered Lindsey and turned back for her. A man who had frequently teased and tickled her now presented a face carved from granite. Only the tears that trickled down his cheeks betrayed him.

The crowd, awakened from their stunned silence, began to murmur, a rising wave of excited sound. Lindsey's mother had ceased to scream, and kept asking in a dull monotone, 'Did anyone see a parachute? Was there a 'chute?' In the background, ambulances screamed their cries of distress, and helicopters started up, their enormous blades slowly clanking and then whirling about faster and faster until they whined in high-pitched protest as they sliced through the air. And sliced through Lindsey's head. The roaring in her ears intensified and she wanted to cover them. An enormous force pressed on her chest, preventing her from breathing. She began to gasp for air. The whining grew louder and louder. Why wouldn't it stop? She couldn't stand it any more.

Lindsey Keegan was eight years old.


'Smoking or non-smoking?' The woman behind the airline counter asked the question automatically, her public smile pasted firmly in place.

'Non-smoking.'

'Window seat?'

'No, and I want to sit as far back in the tail as I can.'

Surprised out of her mechanical routine, the clerk looked with new interest at the passenger standing before her. Several inches over five feet, with short, golden-blonde hair that curled about her lovely face, and clad in a chic brown trouser suit, the woman stared back, a challenging look in her wide-set avocado-green eyes. 'In the tail?' the clerk repeated uncertainly.

'Yes.'

'That's stupid. The tail is the bumpiest place to ride.' At a gesture from the clerk, Ross tossed her suitcases, one at a time, on to the scales. 'Give her a seat over the wing. You'll have a much smoother ride there, Lindsey.'

'I believe I'm the one who has to get on that plane, Ross, not you. I'll ride where I want.' Lindsey turned back to the ticket agent who was trying to give a good imitation of a woman who was not fascinated by the discussion before her. 'I'll have an aisle seat, and in the tail,' she reiterated.

Unable to help herself, the clerk said diffidently, 'He's right, you know. Most people prefer to sit over the wings.'

'And spend the whole trip watching the engines to see if the propellers will fall off? No, thank you,' replied Lindsey firmly.

'You're travelling on a jumbo jet. They don't have propellers,' Ross pointed out.

'All right; so I'd have to watch to make sure that they didn't catch fire.'

'You're being ridiculous!'

'And you're being a busybody. If I prefer to ride in the tail, that's my own business,' said Lindsey crossly.

'Give me one good reason why you think it's better to ride in the tail.'

'Well, if you must know,' she said, goaded into an answer she preferred not to give, 'it seems to me that every time there's an airplane crash, the tail breaks off and the only people who survive are those who were sitting there.'

'That's the dumbest thing I ever heard of.'

'You shouldn't have asked.' Taking her ticket back from the agent, and gathering up the baggage claim slips, Lindsey turned away from the counter. 'I don't know why you insisted on driving me to Denver, anyway. All you've done since we left Colorado Springs is whine about my going to Germany.'

'I was not whining,' Ross denied stiffly.

'I don't know what else you'd call it. You've been griping and complaining ever since I told you I was going!' She stuck her boarding pass and ticket in her bag, checking once again in the process to make sure that she had her passport.

'I have not been griping. I merely suggested that it would have been nice if you'd discussed this trip with me before you'd irrevocably committed yourself. I had plans for us this spring.'

'I don't recall ever giving you the right to make any plans for me, Ross,' she said calmly enough, although inside she was seething at the resurrection of a topic which had been discussed endlessly over the past couple of weeks.

'We've been dating for several months now. Naturally I assumed that my regard for you was reciprocated.'

The genuine hurt and bewilderment in his voice lessened Lindsey's annoyance. Struggling to cope with her own fears and anxieties, perhaps she had been a little harsh in her recent treatment of him. Before she could apologise, he continued.

'I never would have thought that you, *especially* you, would hop on a plane just to satisfy some whim.'

Well aware as she was that she had already extensively covered this ground, Lindsey's voice was beginning to have an edge to it. 'I'm hardly going to Europe on a whim! I've explained all this to you a hundred times, and I'm not about to go into it again. Billy and his wife need me.' Spotting her boarding gate number, Lindsey began to walk faster.

'And what about me? I need you!'

Touched at Ross's bald statement, she stopped in her mad dash for the boarding gate and turned to look at him. His fiery red hair stood in tufts where he'd run his hands through it, while pale blue eyes glared down at her.

'I think that's the nicest thing you've ever said to me! I won't be gone long. Less than a month.'

He wasn't appeased. 'You know very well that I was counting on you being in the gallery next week for the golf tournament at my club. Watching it would have helped your own game.'

Irritated that a golf tournament was his top priority at a time like this, she was cool in her answer. 'Can it possibly have escaped your notice, Ross Waverly, that I do not play golf?'

'I know you don't now, but naturally—that is—after—well, this is certainly not the time nor place to talk about our future,' he pontificated.

'I couldn't agree with you more,' concurred Lindsey weakly. A marriage proposal was more than she could cope with at present. It was with relief that she saw that they had reached the door through which passengers were being screened, and through which, fortunately, Ross was not allowed.

Not one to make a spectacle of himself in public, Ross pecked her on the cheek, gave her a number of last-minute instructions which she had no intention of following, and started to turn away. Lindsey fumbled in her bag for her ticket and boarding pass, blinking back tears that appeared from out of nowhere. She wondered if the tears were a sign that she liked Ross more than she realised, or if they were merely a barometer of her distress over the forthcoming trip.

Slowly Lindsey handed over her ticket to the attendant and entered the boarding area. Oblivious to her surroundings, she dropped into the first vacant seat. When she had first met Ross, she had been attracted to him. Slow and steady, always self-assured, he was an anchor that could keep her more impetuous personality firmly on the ground. A lawyer in her stepfather's firm, he came from an old-established Colorado family. Years ago, Waverlys had entertained General Palmer, the founder of Colorado Springs, and today Ross's parents were on first name terms with the Mayor and most of the city council. The house where Ross was raised had been built back when Colorado Springs was a mere resort visited by rich Easterners. It wasn't his money or his family's prominence, however, which had appealed to Lindsey, but his stability and the sense of security that he gave her.

Now, however, she began to wonder if Ross's stability had been his only appeal. Certainly he had not been very understanding about the fact that when someone in her family needed her, she had no choice but to respond. Helen had no family of her own to help out, and even if Billy was only her stepbrother, he had always been there for her. Perhaps she wasn't being fair to Ross. Admittedly her emotional state was such that she was in no condition to make any decisions at all these days. As the time of her departure approached, Lindsey had been haunted by her fears. Although she had often flown as a child, from the time of her father's death she had not been near a plane. Even more debilitating was the fact that her mother was aware of her phobia and felt so guilty about her daughter going in her place that Lindsey had to pretend that she had outgrown her fear of flying. The result was night after night of hideous nightmares where she re-lived every moment of her father's fiery crash.

While on the outside she might look perfectly calm, by the time Ross had delivered her to Denver's Stapleton Airport she had been a bundle of nerves and banked hysteria. No wonder he had so easily irritated her.

Lindsey looked at her watch. Still some time to go before departure. She berated herself at letting her irritation with Ross get the best of her. If she had been more understanding of his complaints she could be sitting in an airport lounge having something to calm her agitated nerves.

On the other side of a large expanse of glass Lindsey could see the waiting plane. How could anything that large even get off the ground? Once again she cursed the circumstances that were forcing her to board the monster that squatted out there. It wasn't Helen's fault that the doctors had determined that a Caesarean section operation was necessary with this pregnancy, and certainly, both Helen and Billy had been as astounded as anyone when the doctors had announced that she was carrying twins. Until Charles's unexpected heart attack, Lindsey's mother and stepfather had planned to go to Germany to help Helen out, looking forward to their trip with great anticipation. Luckily Charles's attack had been minor, and he was home and recovering nicely, but a trip to Europe was out of the question. Naturally, Caroline could not go off and leave Charles at home alone. That had left only Lindsey. A frantic rush had ensued. Passport pictures were taken and the passport sent for. Details at work had been quickly ironed out. Her partners at the shop were not only very understanding, they envied her the trip to Europe. Little did they know.

Involuntarily her eyes were drawn back to the sleek, shining jet which perched outside the window. To Lindsey's overheated imagination the huge plane resembled nothing more than an enormous bird of prey waiting with calm inevitability to gobble her up. She shut her eyes. She mustn't let her imagination run away with her. All she was going to do was get on the plane and fly across the ocean. People did it every day and thought nothing of it. People who weren't named Lindsey Keegan did it. Why hadn't she listened to Charles when he had recommended that she take tranquillisers? Years had passed since the accident, but it was imprinted on her mind as vividly as if it had occurred five minutes ago. She could still smell the hamburger rotting in the hot sun, see the black mushroom of smoke, hear the boom of the crash and the cries of the crowd . . .

'Easy does it. We're off the ground now.'

Slowly Lindsey forced open her eyelids, looking up into the brightest blue eyes she had ever seen. Encased in a network of fine squint lines, they were filled with concern and anxiety. She shook her head to try and erase the lingering blur of her memories. 'I . . . I . . .' Vivid recollections of her father's accident still held her in their grip, and she was helpless to speak.

Ignoring her stuttering efforts, the man said calmly, 'While I'm always happy to hold the hand of an attractive woman, do you suppose you could remove your fingernails from my skin?'

Dazed, Lindsey looked down to where she held the man's hand in a death grip in her lap, her two hands clenching his so hard that her knuckles shone white, while her nails bit deeply into his flesh. Her eyes flew to a window where a wisp of white cloud brushed against the glass and was gone, leaving only blue to be seen. Fear rose in waves to her throat. Swallowing convulsively, she turned disbelieving eyes back to the man beside her. 'I don't understand. What happened?' How could she have missed leaving the boarding area and getting on the plane?

'Nothing happened,' he said in soothing tones. 'We took off, and the plane is working just fine. Are you okay? Lindsey closed her eyes, her heart pounding sickeningly against her ribs. Concentrating on slowing down her rapid breathing, she ignored his question.

'Can I have the stewardess bring you something?' he asked urgently.

Shaking her head, Lindsey answered hoarsely, 'No, no. I'll be fine in a minute.' Operating strictly by willpower, she brought her fears under some semblance of control. Gradually her breathing became almost normal, and her racing pulse beat slowed.

A shifting of the man's arm brushed it up against her breast, reminding her that she still held his hand imprisoned in her lap. Hastily she let go, giving an involuntary gasp at the deep half-moons imprinted on his hand by her nails.

'I'd venture to say that you don't care for flying.' Amusement mingled with concern in his voice. Lindsey ventured a quick peep up at him; his eyes were warm with sympathy and compassion.

'Is it so obvious?' She smiled weakly at him. The realisation that she'd surmounted the first obstacle of her trip lifted her spirits and sent a shot of courage through her vein.

The man grinned. 'Lucky guess,' he teased her. With a meaningful look, he rubbed his injured hand.

Ashamed of her loss of control, Lindsey muttered a swift apology.

'Don't worry about it. One time I flew beside a lady who threw up with every landing and take-off. Having my hand held is infinitely preferable, believe me.' He punctuated his statement with a cocky grin that forced an answering smile from Lindsey. 'Hey, that's not your next act, is it?' he asked with visible horror.

'I don't think so,' she said, adding honestly, 'However, I haven't flown since I was eight.' She looked down at her hands still clenched in her lap. 'You must think I'm a fool.'

'Well, I must admit when you first grabbed my hand I thought it was a novel way for a woman to pick up a man.'

'You didn't?' she asked in chagrin, a red flush crawling up her neck.

'I did. However,' he went on, 'that stranglehold you got on my wrist soon rid me of any notions that you were devastated by my charm.'

'I'm so embarrassed,' moaned Lindsey.

Fortunately for her, the flight attendant at that point took over the loudspeaker and began giving emergency instructions. Although Lindsey had little faith that masks falling from over her head or windows that could be popped out would be of any use to her in an emergency, she listened attentively. Obediently she read the added information in the booklet in the seat pocket as the stewardess instructed. It remained a mystery to her how she could have given out her boarding pass and walked on to a plane and taken a seat, presumably speaking to people in the process, and have absolutely no recollection of doing so.

'You were rather absent-minded when you first sat down. I thought perhaps you were thinking of the boy-friend you left behind.' Her seat mate had evidently decided she'd read enough.

'Boy-friend?' She was pleased that her voice was returning to normal.

'The red-haired fellow who decided he'd ask you to marry him some other time.' At her look of outrage, he added, 'I was standing behind you in line. Are you going to say yes when he finally pops the question?'

'While I admit that I may have somewhat—er—infringed upon you during take-off, I don't see where that gives you the right to quiz me on my personal life.' There. That cool tone should settle his hash.

'If I were a more sensitive person, I'd probably recognise that as a snub.' His tone clearly invited her to laugh with him.

'You're unbelievable!' She fought the urge to smile, but a traitorous dimple gave her away.

His eyes had been watchful, but now they relaxed at her smile. He stuck out his hand. 'Cole Farrell. Be careful when you shake that hand. It's been recently injured.'

'You're not going to let me forget my neurotic behaviour, are you?'

'I'll make a deal. You tell me about yourself and keep me entertained, and I'll say no more about our—er—painful introduction.'

'Entertain you? What are you, a child?'

'Nope. Just a man who forgot to buy a good book in the airport, and who now, faced with a beautiful woman, is trying to make the most of his opportunity.'

It was impossible not to be amused. 'You're outrageous!' she laughed.

'And you are avoiding telling me your name.'

'You win. Lindsey Keegan.' She shook, very gently, the proffered hand.

'Nice to meet you, Lindsey Keegan.' Laughing lights danced in his eyes as he accepted her hand. 'Where are you headed?'

Firmly she extracted her fingers which he seemed to forget he was holding. 'I'm on my way to Germany.'

'I'd venture to guess that you're not merely a tourist. Anyone with a phobia about flying like yours must have a pretty strong reason for going overseas.'

'The strongest,' Lindsey affirmed. 'Someone very special to me needs me. And where are you going?'

A whimsical smile twisted his firm lips. 'Would you believe that I'm headed for Germany, too?'

'No, are you really? How nice,' she ended lamely. Aware that her initial enthusiasm had deepened the laugh lines around his eyes, she buried herself in the flight magazine pulled from the seat pocket in front of her. To her relief, he accepted her retreat, and turned to stare out of the window. Endless moments later the flight attendant came down the aisle passing out newspapers, and she and Cole Farrell each accepted one. Silence reigned, marred only by the rustling of turning pages. Finishing hers, Lindsey was about to ask him if he cared to swap, when without warning, the plane took a sudden and startling dive. Her stomach dropped to her toes. Instinctively her hand shot out and clenched his arm. 'What happened?' she asked, her voice quavering with fear.

Patting her hand, he tried to reassure her. 'It was just an air pocket. Happens all the time. Nothing to be concerned with. But just to be on the safe side, keep your seat belt fastened as long as we're in the air.'

'You mean . . . you mean it could happen again?'

'It could. Air isn't a stable commodity, you know. All kinds of factors can produce a little turbulence. It's nothing to worry about.'

'Nothing for you to worry about, you mean,' she retorted. 'It's plenty for me to worry about.'

He folded up his newspaper and putting it aside, removed her hand from his arm and turned it palm up. Peering down at her from beneath hooded eyes he traced his finger lightly over her open palm. 'Your life line tells me that you will live many more years. I see world travel and a handsome stranger,' he predicted in a hoarse whisper.

'Tall, dark and handsome, I hope.' Lindsay shivered at his sensuous touch.

'Tall, handsome and semi-dark.' Meaningfully he inclined his own brown head.

'Oh.' With a great show of disappointment, she tugged on her hand until he released it. 'I had my heart set on a tall, dark stranger.'

'Woman, you are hard to please. However,' he craned his neck past her and peered down the aisle, 'you're in luck. Three seats ahead of you is exactly the man you seek.'

Following the direction of his gaze, Lindsey looked past the row of seats to where a black-haired toddler bounced with excitement on his mother's lap. 'Ah, dark and handsome, yes. But what happened to tall?'

'You really are greedy, aren't you?'

'You're the gypsy fortune-teller, not me. When you promise me tall, I expect tall.'

Laughing at their nonsense, they were barely aware when the attendant exchanged their papers for a tray of food. Passing from silly topics to serious, they were soon chatting away like old friends. Lindsey realised that Cole was doing all in his power to divert her thoughts from the flight, and she was grateful for his kindness.

The time passed more quickly than Lindsey would have thought it could, and soon the attendant was giving the landing instructions for New York. The inside of Lindsey's mouth went dry, and she forgot completely what they were talking about. Tamped-down fears began rising acidly in her throat as she stared blindly ahead.

Without a word, Cole checked to make sure her seat belt was snug, and then, putting a tweed-clad arm around her, he gathered her close to him. With a gulping sob,

Lindsey buried her face in his shoulder, her body shaking uncontrollably. She could feel the pressure building explosively in her ears, the hurtling descent of the plane. At the thud of the landing gear dropping, she clutched Cole's hand tighter. He murmured soft words of encouragement in her ear as the plane bounced upon the runway. The deep roar of the engines assaulted her ears.

Suddenly there was blissful peace. The roaring stopped, and the plane rolled to a stop. Around them Lindsey could hear little bustling noises as people prepared to embark, the voices sounding loud outside the small oasis of silence where she and Cole sat.

Shakily she pulled away from him, averting her eyes in embarrassment. He would be happy to see the last of her.

Capable hands dispensed with her seat belt. 'Two down and two to go,' Cole's deep voice rumbled.

Lindsey looked up at him. Expecting to see pity or amusement on his face, she was confused and flustered by the warm look of admiration.

'Here we are in New York,' she said gamely, inwardly praying that her boneless legs would support her when she stood.

'Attagirl!' Cole's fist lightly brushed her jaw in a gesture of approval. Standing up, he stepped in front of her and gathered her belongings from the overhead compartment. 'I assume that we're on the same flight to Frankfurt.'

Lindsey dipped into her bag, and pulling out her ticket, compared it with his. 'Yes, we are.'

'Good. We have a couple of hours here before departure. What would you say to a drink?'

'What would a drowning man say to a life preserver?' she shot back.

He laughed. 'I take it that means yes.' A firm hand in

the small of her back, he guided her down the narrow aisle.

A short time later, Lindsey leaned back in the plush chair and took a deep sip of the wine that Cole handed her.

'Here's to the second leg of our journey. May it be as pleasant as the first.' He toasted her with his glass.

'I don't ask for pleasant,' she reminded him. 'All I ask for is that I get there in one piece.'

A slow smile crinkled up the corners of Cole's eyes. 'You never did tell me what's so important that you would risk life and limb, at least in your opinion, to get to Germany.'

'My brother is stationed in the Air Force at Rhein-Main Air Base, and I'm going over there to help out his wife, Helen. She just gave birth to twins.'

'That would be Bill and Helen Jeffries, I'd guess.'

'You know Billy?' asked Lindsey in delight.

'You could say that; he's my squadron commander. Wait a minute—you said your last name was Keegan. Did I miss a husband somewhere?'

Lindsey smiled. 'Hardly. My mother married Billy's father after my own father died. I never think of Billy as a stepbrother. Even though he's so much older than me, we've always been close.'

'Lucky girl,' said Cole lightly.

'Yes,' Lindsey said soberly, 'I know I am. That's why I have to go and help Billy out now. It couldn't have been easy for him having a little sister thrust on him when he was already twenty-three. I idolised him and followed him everywhere. He didn't have a bit of privacy when he came home, and he never once complained. Having lost my father, far from resenting Billy, I smothered him. Looking back on it now, I don't know how he managed to put up with me.'

'I bet you were a cute little kid,' he teased. 'All curls and big eyes, just like Shirley Temple.'

'Don't you believe it,' she retorted. 'No frilly dresses for me. I was a regular tomboy: pig tails and Band-aids were my normal attire.'

Cole laughed and then called her attention to the loudspeaker making an announcement about their flight. Much as Lindsey hated to leave the warm security of the lounge, she followed Cole to the plane, where they managed to secure seats together. This time she was determined to conquer her fears, and as the plane taxied down the runway she was pleased to hear only a small tremor in her voice as she asked Cole questions about his life in Germany.

Waiting for their turn to take off, Cole did his best to channel her thoughts away from their flight by telling humorous stories about his work. Although he was a pilot, his stories dealt with people rather than planes, for which Lindsey was grateful.

As the plane's engines grew louder, and the huge machine began speeding down the runway, Lindsey's fears re-surfaced, and her heart began to race with alarm. She felt the plane lift off; the giant pressure was forcing her back against her seat and choking off her efforts to breath. She gasped for air and inhaled the comforting male scent of aftershave and musk. Her face was buried in Cole's shoulder. Ashamed that once again she had made an idiot of herself, Lindsey muttered a broken apology.

'Only a fool would object to a beautiful woman clinging to him,' Cole assured her. 'No one's ever called me a fool,' he added softly.

Although the thought of all that icy water beneath them made her slightly ill, Lindsey did her best to concentrate on conversing with Cole. On this flight dinner was served, and they laughed as they argued about what they were eating. Lindsey voted for fricasseed eel, while Cole swore it was barbecued rattlesnake. Over coffee he asked her what she did for a living.

'I'm a fibre artist,' she told him.

'A what?'

'Fibre artist. That's a fancy way of saying that I make things out of material. Not necessarily clothes, although I do make those, too. Mostly I make wall hangings, with some pillows and toys for an occasional diversion.'

'And you make money doing that?'

'Well, not a lot,' she admitted, 'although crafts are more and more being considered an art form the same as oil paintings and watercolours. Actually, what keeps the wolf at bay is our gallery.'

'Gallery?' he queried.

'Uh-huh. When I graduated from college last year armed with a degree in fine arts—well, employers didn't exactly beat a path to my door. One night several of us in the same position got to talking and decided if no one else would take a chance on us, it was up to us. So we opened our own store to sell our own things.'

'Just like that?'

'Well, not quite just like that,' she conceded. 'Banks weren't as impressed by the idea as we were, so we all had to borrow from relatives. We gathered a few more interested parties until there were six of us, found an empty store that wasn't too far off the beaten path, filled it with our own things, and browbeat any talented friends to let us sell their creations on consignment. One thing led to another, and now the Wild Iris, if not exactly making us all millionaires, is at least operating in the black. And, best of all, we retained the idea of it being a consignment shop, so the overhead stays low. Then, with six of us, we each only work two days a week. That's how

I can get off now. I'll just owe everyone for the days they worked for me.'

'Sounds like quite an enterprise,' Cole said in admiration. 'What did you call the shop?'

'The Wild Iris. We came up with the idea of the store in the spring just before graduation. It had been an abnormally wet winter, and the wild irises were prolific that year. That seemed a hopeful sign—you know, the earth showing fruit and all that. It may sound silly, but we thought it was a pretty name.'

'I really am impressed. It must have taken a lot of gumption for you to go out on your own like that.'

'Don't get too impressed. We were just too stupid to know any better. And luck had a lot to do with it,' she admitted. 'Our timing was just right, as crafts are really popular these days; one of the gals was dating a newspaper man so we got some free publicity; and, best of all, the area where we built has started picking up lots of tourist trade.'

'Are all your partners women?'

'Yes. That wasn't intentional, it just kind of happened, but it's worked out well. We get along with a surprising lack of disagreement, and working only two days a week, even the ones who got married have stuck to the shop, so we still have the original six partners.'

While they had been talking, the sky outside had blackened, the movie which they had both already seen was over, and now the main cabin lights were turned off. As the other passengers restlessly settled down for the night, Cole handed Lindsey her blanket and a small pillow. 'A big day for you tomorrow. Maybe you'd better get some sleep.'

'Are you kidding? There's no way I'm going to fall asleep. What if the pilot should need me for something?' she asked, half in jest, but she lay down obediently.

Peach-coloured threads of dawn were lacing the night skies when Lindsey opened her eyes. All around her she could hear little noises and low murmurs of conversation as the other passengers gradually awakened. Warm and comfortable, the flight blanket tucked snug beneath her chin, Lindsey was content to sit quietly for the moment. Gradually it was borne in upon her that the pillow under her head was quite firm and rather scratchy. A slight turn of her head confirmed her suspicions. Some time during the night she had discarded her pillow and substituted Cole's tweed-clad shoulder. Hastily she sat erect, colour warming her face as she saw that he was awake and watching her. 'I'm sorry. You should have pushed me off!' she exclaimed.

'Don't be silly. I've been the envy of every man who walked past during the night. Your cuddling up to me like that put quite a feather in my cap.'

'It might have put a feather in your cap, but it looks like it also put a crick in your shoulder,' Lindsey retorted as she noticed him try surreptitiously to flex stiff muscles.

'Guilty as charged. Usually when I have a beautiful woman in my arms, I'm not concerned with trying not to waken her. Just the opposite, as a matter of fact.'

Unable to come up with a snappy reply, Lindsay was thankful that the stewardess came up at that moment serving them their continental breakfasts. There wasn't much time for conversation after that as she freshened up in the wash-room and then gathered her belongings together. 'Are we about there?' she asked.

Cole craned his head towards a window. 'Just a few minutes. I can see the new runway from here.'

'A few minutes!' She clenched her bag, her eyes shut. She hated the landings worst of all: the noise; that awful bump when the plane hit the ground. Cole took one trembling hand in his large one and squeezed reassuring-

ly. She needed no encouragement to burrow deep into the
sanctuary of his arms again.

True to Cole's prediction, only a few moments passed
before they were safely rolling along the ground.
Straightening up and releasing her pent-up breath,
Lindsey looked towards the far window where she could
catch glimpses of trees and buildings rushing past.
Shakily she released her death grip on Cole's hand. 'Here
we are,' she announced unnecessarily. Although the
plane had not yet come to a complete halt, passengers
were already streaming down the aisles. Somewhat to her
surprise, Lindsey was reluctant to join the exodus
towards the door. Cole's patient understanding and lively
companionship had been her salvation throughout the
journey. She hated to say goodbye.

As if he sensed her thoughts Cole growled out of the
corner of his mouth, 'Stick with me, babe, I'll get you out
of this mess.'

Laughing at his terrible gangster imitation and
grateful that he wasn't abandoning her yet, Lindsey
preceded him into the aisle. They passed through what
seemed to her a bewildering array of tunnels and
corridors before a bored passport control officer waved
them past him.

'He barely looked at it,' Lindsey complained. 'I
thought we were supposed to get grilled and all that. He
didn't even stamp my passport!'

Cole laughed. 'He just doesn't know a dangerous
woman when he sees one.'

She was thankful for Cole's guiding arm as they
walked through Frankfurt's large, bustling terminal. The
bright lights and so many people scurrying in all
directions left her feeling lost and confused. A loudspeaker broadcast announcements in several languages,
and dogs could be heard wildly barking. Startled by a

beep behind her, she stood frozen until Cole pulled her from the path of an onrushing cart. Before she could thank him a bicycle flashed by on her right. 'Do you have any idea where we're going?' she asked.

'Sure. I've been here lots of times.' He gave her a commiserating smile. 'It is pretty confusing the first time.'

In the baggage area, she was again grateful for his experience as he quickly secured baggage carts and led her to the luggage carousel. The suitcases had not yet appeared, so they stood to one side, chatting quietly. Lindsey kept waiting for Cole to mention seeing her again, but to her chagrin, he spoke only of the sights she must see, the food she must try, and the places she must visit. Pride kept her from bringing up the subject herself. He was probably relieved to be seeing the last of such a coward. Suddenly it occurred to her that she had never asked Cole if he were married. He wasn't wearing a ring, but that meant little.

When the luggage finally arrived, Cole heaved hers on to a cart and pushed it to the Customs line. 'Your brother will be right through those double doors,' he promised. 'Take it easy for the next few days. Jet lag can really get you down.' A light kiss on her cheek and he was gone, back to find his own bags.

Waved past by the Customs guard, Lindsey went through the doors and looked in panic at the large crowd milling about. How would she ever find Billy?

He found her. Arms grabbed her around the waist and swung her about. Breathless, she looked up into her stepbrother's spectacled, grinning face. 'Good lord, kid, you get better-looking every day! I'm going to have to keep you under lock and key or else I'll spend all my time beating off woman-hungry bachelors!'

Lindsey hugged him tightly. It was so good to see him

again. She had so many things to ask him, so much to tell.

'How's . . .?' they both burst out together, and then stopped to laugh with the sheer pleasure of their reunion.

'You first,' Billy said.

'How's Helen and the twins?'

'Doing great. In fact, they'll be home tomorrow. That doesn't give you much chance to rest before the invasion, I'm afraid.'

'I don't care; I can hardly wait to see them, and Helen, too.' She looked around. 'Where are Paddy and Charlie? I thought they'd come with you?'

'They wanted to, but I wasn't sure how long I'd have to wait. They're at a neighbour's, watching cartoons.'

By this time Billy had wheeled her luggage across to a car park and was loading it in the boot of his car. With a tired sigh, Lindsey sank on to the soft front seat.

Billy joined her. 'Thought I might see a friend of mine with you.'

'Oh. Why's that?'

'A fellow in my squadron went out to Colorado for an interview, and I told him what flight you'd be on and asked him to try and get on the same one.' He reached over and patted her hand. 'Knowing how much you hate to fly, Helen and I really appreciate your coming over here to help us out. I don't know what we would have done without you.' He shifted gears and backed the car out of the car park. 'I asked Cole to take care of you. I thought having someone with you might make the trip a little easier for you.'

'Cole Farrell?' Lindsey asked.

Billy was concentrating on the traffic and he missed her start of surprise at the mention of Cole's name. 'Then you did meet him?'

'Yes, I did. He . . . he was very kind. Thank you for thinking of it.'

'Knew I could count on Cole,' Billy said in satisfaction.

Lindsey turned to stare dully out of the window, a sinking feeling in the pit of her stomach. Cole had known all along who she was. Standing behind her in line, he had probably seen her name on her ticket and requested the seat next to hers. No wonder he hadn't bothered to suggest seeing her again. His interest in her had been based purely on doing a favour for a friend; Billy had asked him to take care of her. Well, she couldn't complain; he had done his job well. A lone tear slipped down her cheek, and she quickly brushed it away before Billy saw it.

# CHAPTER TWO

MOTHERHOOD was certainly not all it was cracked up to be, Lindsey thought grimly as she brushed her hair back off her forehead with a flour-dusted hand, leaving a streak of white. Her nerves were teetering on the razor edge of shattering. Thinking to occupy four busy hands which had already made a mockery of her morning's house-cleaning efforts, and at the same time keep the boys quiet so their mother and the twins could sleep, Lindsey had suggested that they bake cookies. No one in her right mind would have have thought of doing an enterprise so fraught with disaster, although there was no question that the boys had enjoyed their cooking spree. The flour all over the floor could attest to their enthusiasm—not to mention the hunks of raw dough!

Lindsey looked about the kitchen in disbelief. How could one adult and two small boys create a such a mess? Thankfully two of the perpetrators were safely ensconced in the bathtub. She could hear them merrily splashing away through the open door. Meanwhile cookie crumbs littered the floor, there were splashes of dough dribbled down the front of the cabinets, and dirty dishes were piled everywhere. A quick glance at the clock did nothing to raise her spirits. Helen would soon be waking, the twins would be shouting to be changed and fed, and Billy would be home demanding his dinner any minute now.

That last thought spurred her into motion. As she wiped down the kitchen she thought wryly that it was probably a good thing that Cole Farrell hadn't been

29

interested in seeing her again. She didn't know when she would have fitted him in. She thought of his engaging smile and warm blue eyes. Who was she kidding? She'd have found time. Just her luck that he hadn't found her as attractive as she'd found him. She had tried to convince herself that no man would have been that friendly unless he'd had some interest in her, but as almost a week had passed since her arrival and Cole had made no effort to get in touch with her, she had been forced to admit that his attentions had been solely as a favour to Billy. Not that she could blame him for being reluctant to pursue an acquaintance with her, considering her behaviour on the plane trip.

Fifteen minutes later she sighed with relief. Most of the dishes were in the dishwasher, the cabinets were wiped clean, and a pot of spaghetti sauce bubbled busily away on the stove.

Shouts from the bathroom sent her on the fly. She was just in time to grab a toppling Charlie from the edge of the tub. A short scold, and the two boys were dried off and sent to their rooms to dress. She considered changing her own dough-spattered clothing, but at that moment the male half of the Jeffries twin-set awoke and quickly awakened his sister. Changing one set of nappies and then the other, stopping only to help with Charlie's shoelaces and Paddy's reluctant zipper, she congratulated herself on finally getting things under control. Handing the babies to a still-drowsy Helen, she quickly warmed the bottles.

It was a relief to have an excuse to sit and rest while she fed Mandy, the female half of the Jeffries twins. Moments like this made her envy Helen her role as wife and mother. When chubby little fists waved in the air, she forgot the spilled milk and the scattered flour. Allowing her mind to drift, she saw herself in her own house, painted blue to match Cole's eyes. Now where had that preposterous thought come from? Looking down at Mandy she visualised her as a little boy, a miniature of Cole. Cole, Cole! She had to get that man out of her mind. It was ridiculous to moon over a man just because he'd done her a kindness at her brother's request.

Paddy's solemn face in the doorway brought her back to reality. 'Auntie Lin, something smells funny in the kitchen.'

'Oh no, the spaghetti sauce!' Jumping up hastily, she dislodged the bottle from Mandy's mouth, and the tiny infant was quick to protest. Lindsey hastened to the kitchen, at the same time attempting to persuade Mandy to accept the teat again. The baby preferred to squall. Disaster greeted Lindsey in the kitchen. Black smoke poured from the empty pan the water for the pasta had been boiling in. Reluctantly she checked the sauce. Her worst fears were confirmed, the odour enough to convince anyone that it was burned beyond human consumption.

The sight of Charlie nonchalantly munching cookies, forbidden this close to his dinner hour, was the last straw. Holding the squalling infant close, she marched over to Mandy's brother. Charlie, in his haste to replace what was left of the cookie, without removing his eyes from Lindsey, knocked the cookie jar and all its contents to the floor, where the jar smashed into a thousand pieces, the china bits indistinguishable from the crumbs of what had been several dozen cookies. Charlie burst into tears, and Mandy wailed louder.

'What's going on here?' Billy rushed into the kitchen and flung open the window. One look showed him the offending culprits and he dashed to remove the pans from the stove. 'This probably isn't a good time to ask if that was dinner.' He reached for the baby, who promptly showed favouritism by immediately ceasing to cry.

'It's not funny!' Lindsey was on the verge of tears herself.

'Can I do something to help?' A concerned face peered around Billy's. 'I can hear Helen calling from the other room.'

'Oh no!' Lindsey cried. 'What are you doing here?'

Cole raised a questioning brow. 'I thought I was invited to dinner.'

'To dinner!' she echoed in dismay, looking around her. 'Oh no,' she moaned again, well aware how she must look, surrounded by disaster, her clothes painted with food and baby stains, her hair white with flour, and tears clinging to her lashes. Did this man always have to see her at her worst?

Billy frowned on his way out of the kitchen. 'Didn't Paddy tell you I phoned that Cole was coming home for dinner?'

'No.' Paddy would be lucky if he lived to see six.

'Paddy!' The stern voice brought his son at once. 'I thought I told you when I called to tell Auntie Lin that I was bringing company home for dinner.'

Paddy hung his head. 'I forgot.'

'How could you forget? All you had to do was run and tell her.'

'But it was at the exciting part of the cartoon, and I was going to tell her later, only . . .' He could see that his excuse was not cutting it with his father. 'I'm sorry, Daddy,' he added in a woebegone voice.

'No cartoons for you the rest of the week, young man,' his father instructed in a firm voice. 'Maybe next time you'll be more responsible about carrying out your duties.'

'Yes, Daddy.'

'Now go tell your mother I'll be right in.' Billy sent the

small boy on his way with a well-placed swat.

'Maybe it would be best if I came back another time,' Cole suggested tactfully.

'No, I want to settle that problem we were talking about earlier.' He turned to Lindsey. 'Just leave this mess for now. You can clean it up later. Meanwhile why don't you see if you can scare us up something to eat.'

'No!' Lindsey ripped off her apron and flung it across the kitchen. The look of amusement on Cole's face as he looked around the kitchen, combined with Billy's total disregard for her feelings, was like a match to kindling. 'You clean it up later. I've had it with your kids, your kitchen, your friends, and especially you. Night after night you waltz in here demanding that your dinner be on the table. Then, after you feed your face, you collapse in front of the television, never considering that I might be tired, too. You assume that I want to read to your kids and tuck them into bed. You're spoiled, Billy Jeffries, and if Helen ever decides to divorce you, believe me, I'm on her side. You want dinner tonight? You can just cook it yourself. I quit!' Storming out of the kitchen after her sweeping indictment of her stepbrother, Lindsey was only kept from bursting out with laughter at the thunderstruck faces on the two men she left behind by the fact that she was so angry.

The hot bath, filled with bubbles up to her chin, did much to restore her composure, and slowly the humour of the situation began to grow on her. Once, small knuckles began knocking on the door, but the owner was quickly dragged away by his father before she could answer. Poor Billy. It wasn't his fault that his sister was totally incompetent in the kitchen and equally inept at caring for small children. That scene was just what he didn't need after a long day of shouldering the enormous burden of responsibility that came with his command.

And she had to face the truth. That outburst would never have happened if Cole hadn't been there. There was no denying the quick burst of joy she'd felt when she'd first seen him standing there in the doorway. A joy quickly squelched by the realisation that he hadn't come to see her, but was there to work with Billy. If only she had been calm and cool about the whole situation. Admittedly, it was a little difficult to maintain one's poise in the midst of the disaster in which Cole had found her, but did she have to fly completely off the handle?

She glanced over at the clock. An hour had passed since she'd fled the kitchen. With luck, Billy and Cole had finished their business and Cole had left. She was too embarrassed to face him again. Heaven only knew what she was going to be able to throw together for dinner. Even in the best of times, throwing together was hardly her forte, and this was definitely not the best of times.

A thunderous pounding on the door startled her into dropping the soap. 'You homesteading in there?' Billy called.

'Yes. Go away.'

'I'm sorry about this evening. Can you forgive a thoughtless brother who had his mind on a problem at work and took it out on his favourite sister?'

The humble note in his voice shamed Lindsey. Billy didn't need to apologise; she'd been the one who had thrown the temper tantrum. 'No, no, I should apologise to you, Billy. I don't know what got into me, yelling at you like that. I didn't mean a word of it.'

Billy chuckled. 'I should have remembered that your hair has a streak of red in it.'

'It does not!'

'Come on out and let me show you. We're all starving to death waiting for you so we can eat dinner.'

'Dinner! Oh, Billy, I'm sorry. I ruined dinner.'

'What's the matter? Think you're the only one around here who can cook?'

'Billy,' Lindsey was half laughing and half crying, 'you're the only person I know who could call my efforts cooking.'

'You've got a point,' he conceded. 'Meanwhile, hurry up.'

Lindsey hurried. Throwing on clean slacks and a moss-green blouse that did things for her eyes, she hastily applied her make-up. There was no reason to believe that Cole was still here, she told herself, but that didn't stop her from splashing on a liberal dose of her favourite cologne.

The sight that greeted her as she walked into the dining room brought her to an abrupt halt. Standing in the middle of the kitchen, tasting something on a wooden spoon, was Cole, an enormous dish towel wrapped around his middle. Billy, decked out in an apron that ordered 'Kiss the Cook', was tossing lettuce and tomatoes in a large salad bowl and chatting with Helen who was sitting at the kitchen table sipping a glass of red wine. All traces of Lindsey's disasters had disappeared, swept away by some magical genie. In the dining room itself, the table was set with a clean cloth and what appeared to be Helen's best china.

Billy looked up and saw her. 'Ah! Soaking Beauty arises.'

'What happened?' Lindsey was still astonished at the complete transformation of the kitchen.

Billy looked at her with disgust. 'Lindsey, it may come as some kind of shock to you, but this is the way kitchens are supposed to look. One says "What happened?" when they see a kitchen after you get through with it.'

'Honey, don't tease Lindsey.' Helen moved to the dining room and pointed to the chair across the table from where she was sitting. 'Sit down and let the fellows wait on you for a change. As the ad says, "You deserve a break." '

Lindsey sniffed the air. 'But how in the world did you save the spaghetti sauce? I was sure it was a goner.'

Cole gave her a sideways glance before saying cautiously, 'This is a different sauce.'

'Oh, Helen, I'm sorry. You had to get up and cook.'

'Did you hear that, Cole? This sister of mine is impugning our kitchen talents. We cooked dinner,' he boasted proudly.

'You?' Since Lindsey was well aware that the only person she knew of who cooked worse than she did was her stepbrother, she was extremely sceptical.

'That's what I like—a sister with no faith in one's abilities,' he moaned.

'And in this case she's right,' teased Helen.

'Right. I cannot tell a lie.' He solemnly placed his hand over his heart. 'Cole cooked dinner while I cleaned up the kitchen.'

'Oh.' She looked away from the warm smile that Cole flashed her. It wasn't fair. He could even cook better than she could. The smells coming from the pan he placed on the table were heavenly.

The smells didn't lie. Replete, Lindsey sat back from the table, and accepted a cup of coffee from Billy with a smile. The four adults had enjoyed a delicious dinner and entertaining conversation totally uninterrupted by the four sleeping Jeffries offspring. Her disasters in the kitchen that day seemed light years away.

'Feeling better?' Billy enquired.

'Yes. I must have sounded like a fishwife earlier.'

'You've just been trying to do too much,' Helen scolded. 'We didn't even let you recover from jet lag before the darlings and I came home. And I know those two monsters by the names of Paddy and Charlie have been taking advantage of your good nature and my absorption in the twins to try all their tricks on you, which isn't much of a help.' Ignoring Lindsey's denials, she went on, 'Fortunately Frau Guttmann will be back from her vacation in a couple of days. She's promised to come in twice a week for me and that will be a big help. And I'm feeling much more rested and getting bored in bed, so I can do some of the cooking.'

'And that will be a big help to me,' teased Billy. 'Seriously, what you really need is to get out more. I know you've had the boys to the playground; that's not what I mean. Helen, I don't think that there's anything special coming up this weekend. Are you up to taking care of the fabulous four one day while I take Lindsey for a drive to see a little of the countryside?'

'Certainly. That's a good idea,' Helen agreed, overriding Lindsey's protests.

'I have a better idea.' Cole spoke up in his deep voice. 'You stay home on Sunday and help Helen with your ankle-biters, and I'll take Lindsey for a spin.'

'Done,' agreed Billy before Lindsey had a chance to say anything.

By then it was too late. She had no reason for refusing to go with Cole, and even if she could think of a plausible one, then Billy would insist on taking her and that would leave Helen home to cope with the children. And no matter what Helen said, she was not yet fit enough to do so. Before Cole left, it was settled that he would pick Lindsey up about ten on Sunday morning. She wondered if she would ever stop being an object of charity to Cole.

Lindsey spent the next few days before Sunday bouncing from one emotion to another. One minute she was riding high because Cole had asked her to spend the day with him, the next she was plunged into depression,

aware that he had only asked her as a courtesy to Billy.
And the entire time she scolded herself for caring one
way or the other. Cole was just a man she'd met on a
plane, a pleasant companion, and now he was being kind
enough to show her some of Germany. She would see
some lovely and interesting sights, and he would be fun to
spend the day with. It was ridiculous to expect anything
more.

Nevertheless, on Sunday she dressed with extra care in
a brown split skirt and tweed blazer. Her cream silk
blouse looked versatile enough for any occasion. She was
still trying to decide between several sets of earrings
when she heard Cole at the door. Regretfully setting
aside the gold loops which she felt gave her a more
glamorous air, she inserted small gold balls. A quick dab
of perfume, her raincoat, a splashy tomato red and green
print scarf and she was ready.

Heart thumping, she tried to make a casual entrance
into the living room. Cole was on the floor with Paddy
and Charlie investigating a launch pad they were
building with their small plastic building blocks, but he
looked up as she walked into the room. Suddenly all the
frenzied preparation and indecision were worth it as
Cole surveyed her from head to toe with warm approval.
Lindsey was certain she spied a quick flash of amusement as his eyes rested on her face. 'What's so funny?'
she demanded.

'Later.' He turned to Helen and Billy and after a few
minutes they departed, leaving behind a tearful Paddy
who wanted to accompany them.

'I hope Paddy won't be mad at me for ever,' Cole
remarked lightly as he handed Lindsey into a small,
bright red car.

'No, Paddy doesn't hold a grudge.'

'Good. Because I wanted you all to myself today.' He

slid in under the driver's wheel, then leaned over to help
Lindsey as he saw her struggling with her seat belt. A
quick tug and it was fastened, but he didn't move away,
his face only a couple of inches from hers, an arm resting
on the back of her seat.

The car was small and Cole's shoulders were broad.
Lindsey felt her skin tingling in response to his nearness.
Nervously she tugged at a straying curl. 'There's so much
humidity here that my hair just coils up like a spring', she
complained.

Cole wrapped the curl around his finger, tugging her
head closer. 'I like it.' He leaned nearer, brushing her
chest with the open edges of his corduroy jacket. Lindsey
caught her breath at the contact, uncertain of his
intention. She closed her eyes, blotting out her revealing
mirror-image in his sunglasses. Cole's scent filled her
nostrils and blood pounded in her ears. She felt his warm
breath and a feather-light kiss on the tip of her nose. He
moved away, and she opened her eyes.

Cole was sitting back in his seat, satisfaction written
all over his face. 'I've been wanting to do that since
Thursday night.'

'Why?' she asked, really wondering why that particular spot.

Cole laughed as he smoothly drove from the parking
area. 'That was the only spot on your face not covered
with flour.'

'That's why you were so amused this morning,' she
accused.

'Guilty. Do you mind?'

'Mind? Why should I mind that I constantly make a
fool of myself in front of you? You probably think that
I'm a cowardly, neurotic idiot who shouldn't be allowed
out without a keeper.'

'That's not what I think at all.'

'The way you've seen me behave, how can you think otherwise?' she asked bitterly.

'Easily. First I saw a woman who was terrified to fly, yet in face of that fear, flew clear across the ocean to help out someone who needed her. Then I saw someone who, with a total lack of experience, waded right in and did her best to run a household consisting of two newborns, two unruly little boys, an invalid and a demanding male.'

'Helen can probably do all that with her hands tied behind her back,' sighed Lindsey.

'Helen has also been working up to her present level. She started out with only Bill to deal with, remember? Besides, even Helen sent out an SOS for you,' he pointed out.

'I never thought of it like that. Thanks for the kind words. I've been feeling like a pretty miserable failure.' She gave him a quick glance from beneath lowered lashes. 'It didn't help that your spaghetti sauce was such a hit.'

Cole grinned. 'I had a notion that you wouldn't forgive me for that. Blame it on my grandmother.'

'Your grandmother?'

'She had a small diner down in Del Rio, Texas. I used to spend summers with her. In fact, that's when I decided I was going to be a pilot when I grew up. There's a pilot training base there, and I used to watch the planes flying overhead. Then, too lots of the fellows used to stop by the diner for a bite to eat and I'd listen to them talking. Flying seemed like the most glamorous job in the world to me.'

'And is it?'

He laughed. 'Not exactly. Long hours, no overtime, and for the married guys, lots of time away from home. On the other hand, there's no beating that special feeling I get up there in the air, plus—well, it probably sounds corny to you, but I feel like I'm doing something worthwhile, a service to my country.'

'You must have seen some interesting places?' Lindsey remarked.

He shrugged. 'Some are nothing to write home about, but I have to admit I manage to get around. In fact, I've been TDY ever since I returned from the States.'

'TDY?' Lindsey questioned the unfamiliar term.

'Temporary Duty. A job away from your normal outfit. Whenever we go somewhere overnight, then it's TDY. I went to Berlin the day after I got back and only returned last Thursday.'

The day he had come to Billy's for supper. Lindsey's pulse gave an excited leap. Was he telling her that his absence was why he hadn't called her? She reminded herself that he had come to Billy's because of work and that her presence in his car was directly attributable to the fact that she was his friend's sister. It would be best to be sensible and enjoy the day and her companion without expectations. To that end, she asked politely if he had enjoyed his trip to Berlin.

'No.'

'That's too bad,' she said sympathetically. 'I suppose you were tired after your trip to the States.'

'Not at all,' he denied. 'I was worried about you.'

'About me?' She stared at him in surprise.

'I was worried about whether you were having a good time,' he explained.

'You should have discovered the answer to that on Thursday night,' she retorted.

He grinned, showing perfect white teeth. 'I did, and I can't tell you what a relief that was to me.'

'A relief? To find out how incompetent I am? To discover that I turn into a raving maniac at the drop of a hat?'

'Are you sure you don't mean the drop of a cookie jar?'

'Easy for you to laugh,' she huffed. 'I'd like to see you handle those kids for a week and then see if you can still laugh.'

He ignored her challenge. 'Actually, I wasn't referring to your—er—somewhat disastrous situation. I meant that I was relieved to find out that you hadn't been having a good time, because . . .'

Red sparks erupted in Lindsey's head. 'Of all the outrageous things to say! I'm surprised that you let my brother manoeuvre you into having to put up with me today. Just take me home!'

'Do you always go off half-cocked like this?' Cole asked in comic dismay. 'Before you so rudely interrupted me, I was going to say that I didn't like the idea of you having a good time *without me*. I was afraid that while I was stuck in Berlin the fellows down at the squadron would have booked up all your free time. I've been kicking myself black and blue that I didn't stake my claim before you left the terminal.'

'Oh.' There was silence while Cole concentrated on his driving and Lindsey thought over what he'd said. Finally, her curiosity got the better of her, and she asked, 'Why didn't you?'

'Why didn't I what?'

'You know, what you said. Stake a claim.'

'Oh, that.' He grimaced. 'I didn't want you to feel obligated.'

Lindsey giggled. 'You mean that just because you'd baby-sat me all the way from Colorado, you thought that I might accept a date in return for your kindness?'

'Something like that,' he admitted.

She remembered an earlier grievance. 'Why didn't you tell me that Billy asked you to look out for me on the plane?'

Cole winced. 'I was afraid he'd tell you about that. Believe me, if you weren't so good-looking, I'd have promptly forgotten all about his request, and hidden up in the front of the plane.'

'I don't believe you. You're too nice a person to do that.'

'Oh, no,' exclaimed Cole theatrically. 'You *are* going with me today to pay off a debt, aren't you?'

'Don't be silly. I'm going with you because nobody else asked me,' she teased.

'Boy, are you cruel! What do I have to do to get you to forgive me for laughing at the flour on your face?'

'You can start by telling me where we're going.'

'Up the Rhine, of course. That's where every tourist here has to begin. We're on the *autobahn* to Bingen where we'll pick up the road that runs along the river. We'll drive up the west side for a while, and then return along the east bank. That okay with you?'

'You're the tour guide,' she agreed. She looked out of the window where she could see some hills, blue in the distance. 'I can't believe what a beautiful day it is. I think this is the first day since I've been here that it isn't raining.'

'I hate to tell you this, but March is one of the rainiest months here,' Cole told her.

'Then don't tell me,' begged Lindsey. 'Just let me enjoy today.'

Soon they left the main road and swept through Bingen. Lindsey marvelled at the old buildings. 'Is this the Rhine?' she asked as they crossed a modern bridge.

'No, this is the Nahe River. It runs into the Rhine right here. See, alongside of us.'

Lindsey turned her head quickly from one side to another, anxious to miss none of the fascinating sights. 'We certainly don't have anything like this in Colorado,' she reflected aloud. 'Cole, look.' She pointed to a yellow tower on a small island in the river. 'Is that a castle?'

Looking in the direction she was pointing, Cole shook his head. 'That's the Mouse Tower. It was probably built as some kind of lookout tower. There's a grisly legend attached to it: it seems that an evil bishop shut up all the poor starving people of his district in a barn and then set it on fire. As the fire burned, he laughed at the noises coming from the barn, comparing them to the squeaking of mice. At that, hordes of mice escaped from the barn and chased him to the tower where they supposedly ate him.'

Lindsey shuddered before a castle ruin came into sight, claiming her attention. As they drove along, Cole pointed out one sight after another, always adding a little about the history or legend attached to each. Sometimes he pulled over to the side for her to get a better look. At the small town of Bacharach, they parked and walked around, Lindsey admiring the many quaint half-timbered houses. Her favourite had multiple roofs, one shaped like an upside-down funnel, and writing that Cole translated as meaning 'Old House'. Cole took her into a large shop that was a favourite of Americans, and then, belatedly realising his error, had a terrible time dragging her away from the tempting displays of porcelain.

Until now it had been difficult for Lindsey to believe that she was actually in a foreign country. Staying with Billy and Helen in base housing, all her previous contacts had been with other Americans. For the first time she felt as if she was really in Germany, and she was entranced by all she saw. 'Oh look! I know I've seen pictures of that castle before.'

'Could be,' agreed Cole. 'That's the Pfalzgrafenstein, or simply, Die Pfalz. It was built hundreds of years ago to collect Customs duties from those passing up and down the river. There's a dungeon underneath.' Parking in a small park along the road, he and Lindsey stepped out of the car and walked closer to the river for a better view of the pink and white castle with its five sides and turreted wall. Across the river rose another old castle with an enormous grey tower.

'None of these castles seem to have moats,' complained Lindsey.

'Few in Germany do. Most of the castles are along a river or on a hillside, and that's their defence. In the case of that castle across the river, it wasn't defence enough. Napoleon captured it and wanted it demolished. Luckily, even then some people were concerned about remembering their past, and the man who bought it preserved it. Later it was rebuilt, and it's now a hotel.'

'You must have made this trip a thousand times to know so much about it!'

Cole laughed. 'Would you believe I studied up on it last night?'

'If I were your teacher, I'd give you an A-plus,' Lindsey said, amused and flattered by his admission.

'I'd rather be teacher's pet,' smiled Cole, as he helped her back into his car.

'Greedy,' she mocked, while at the same time her pulse speeded up at the warm look in his eyes.

As they continued along the river, time flew past. Lindsey was discovering again how entertaining Cole could be as he enlightened her about the sights and scenery that they passed. The legend of the Lorelei lost none of its romance as Cole told the story of the bewitching beauty who enchanted sailors with her voice. As Lindsey gazed up at the steep rock which rose high above the river, she could imagine the men so mesmerised by the siren's song that they forgot the dangers of the narrow river and allowed their boats to be dashed to pieces.

At St Goar they boarded an auto-ferry and made it safely across the river to St Goarshausen, Lindsey pretending to be terrified at Cole's outrageous and libellous stories about ferrymen. The day continued fair, and she discovered the truth of Cole's remark that it was easier to see the castles from across the river, noticing several that they had driven beneath earlier but which she had failed to spot. By the time they reached Rüdesheim, she was starving, and grateful when Cole suggested lunch. The season being too early for tourists, they had no problem finding a small café with few patrons. Lindsey panicked when she realised that the menu was in German, but Cole smugly translated it in its entirety before turning it over and showing her that the back side was in English.

After they had ordered, Lindsey following Cole's recommendation, they chatted easily about the sights that they had seen thus far. Cole explained to her some of the different customs of the country, and related some hilarious tales of the misunderstandings that can arise when one is on foreign soil.

'I think you're making half these stories up,' Lindsey disparaged laughingly.

'I swear I'm not, although I'd be tempted to, just to hear you laugh. I'm fascinated by that little gurgle you have in the middle. Before I met you, I never really believed that legend about the Lorelei. It seemed pretty far-fetched that all those sailors could be led astray just by the sound of her voice.'

Embarrassed and pleased by his remark, Lindsey hastily changed the subject. 'What's on the agenda for after lunch, tour guide?'

'Your brother never warned me what a slave driver

you are,' he said plaintively.

By now Lindsey had come to recognise the light in Cole's eyes when he was teasing her, so she was not misled by his tone of voice. 'I'm only here for a short time, and I want to see everything,' she explained.

'A dedicated sightseer,' he said in resignation, sighing loudly for effect.

Lindsey giggled, turning her attention to her lunch which had just been set before her. As they ate, conversation was easy, ranging from their respective careers and families to politics and world headlines. Their opinions didn't always agree, and on occasion they bickered amiably, but Cole was always willing to listen to her views, now and then conceding a point to her. Unlike Ross, the thought came unbidden.

Following lunch they wandered around Rüdesheim, Lindsey enchanted by the narrow Drosselgasse and enticed by the teeming store windows. Giving in at last to temptation, she dragged Cole through the shops while she looked for a present for her mother, settling at last for a Hummel figurine of a small angel. Cole enthusiastically applauded her choice, mostly, she suspected, in relief that she had finally made up her mind.

Standing on the bank of the Rhine, they watched the giant barges slowly forge their way up and down the river. Lindsey was fascinated by the evidence of daily life visible on the barges—children swinging, laundry flapping in the breeze, lace curtains and flowering plants in the windows. In a nearby backwater two swans, their elegant necks held high, swam regally through a crowd of small black coots.

Back in Cole's car, they continued their meandering journey down the river. At Kastel, they again crossed the Rhine, by bridge this time, and entered the large city of Mainz, where they wandered about the main square

admiring the gaily painted buildings. In the cathedral
Lindsey dutifully admired the stained glass windows,
installed after the war. A walk through narrow winding
streets eventually led them to another church.

'I've been showing you the old side of Germany all
day; now you can see a new side,' said Cole as he led her
through the massive doors. Inside the church a chill
emanated from the old stone walls, and after the bright
outdoor sun it seemed dark and dreary until Lindsey
looked in the direction that Cole was pointing and saw
the intense blue of stained glass windows cutting through
the gloom.

'They're gorgeous!' she breathed.

'I thought you'd like them.' Cole's voice was filled with
satisfaction at the pleasure on her face.

'I've never seen anything like them! Wait a minute.
They remind me of something.' Lindsey wrinkled her
brow in concentration. 'I know. One of my friends has a
Chagall reproduction, and it's very similar.'

'There's a good reason for that. These windows are by
Marc Chagall. They're the only Chagall windows in
Germany, as a matter of fact.'

Lindsey slowly walked in front of the altar, gazing up
at the windows which, filled with whimsical figures,
looked like an enormous painting. 'Do you know what
they represent?'

'Sure: Chagall's interpretation of the Bible. See.
There's Noah, Abraham, David . . .' One by one, Cole
pointed out the various stories, Lindsey following
enthusiastically behind.

'I love those yellow angels. These windows are just
glorious. They make me feel—oh, I don't know, joyful.'
She sighed. 'It must be wonderful to be blessed with
talent like that.'

'We can consider ourselves lucky that he lived as long

as he did and left such a fantastic legacy of art to the world. Now with some artists, a shorter life is infinitely preferred,' Cole added with some feeling.

'Like who?' Lindsey immediately challenged, setting off a lively debate about the arts that lasted long past their departure from the church and the city of Mainz. Cole's absurd comments and unorthodox opinions soon had Lindsey weak with laughter.

Settling back against her seat, pleasantly tired from the day's sightseeing, Lindsey surveyed Cole from beneath lowered lashes. Aggressively male, even slouched casually over the steering wheel, Cole exuded an air of competence and quiet confidence. Behind mirrored frames, tiny squint lines added character to his rugged face while his blue eyes matched the good-looking wool turtleneck sweater that he wore beneath a corduroy jacket. From the first moment of their acquaintance, Lindsey had instinctively realised that here was a man to be trusted. Attractive, dependable, amusing, knowledgeable, a great cook, good with kids—it was a shame that she wasn't interested in any man who flew planes for a living.

Back at Billy's apartment, Cole declined an invitation to dinner, pleading an early morning flight. Before he took leave of Lindsey, however, he made arrangements to pick her up for dinner the following evening.

Lindsey loved the little café in his neighbourhood that Cole took her to. As he ate there frequently, the proprietors knew him and made a big fuss over Lindsey. Far from being embarrassed, he showed her off with pride. Soon other regulars drifted in, and all made her feel welcome in their country. Lindsey was impressed by the warmth of Cole's German neighbours, and it was readily apparent to her that these people both liked and respected him.

'I envy you being able to converse in German,' Lindsey said as he drove her home. 'How did you become fluent?'

'Hardly fluent,' Cole denied. 'I took German for several years in college, and that was one of the reasons that I wanted to be stationed over here. I was surprised how it came back once I got here. I still get lost sometimes, especially when they start telling jokes.' He glanced over at her. 'Did you enjoy tonight?'

'I really did. And the food.' She patted her stomach. 'I can see that I'm going to become grossly fat over here!'

Cole's hand reached over and mimicked her actions. 'I can't say that I can feel any excess fat there.'

Her stomach rocked at his touch. She had to fight the urge to press his hand even more intimately against her. As if he sensed her turmoil, Cole smiled lazily down at her before slowly returning his hand to the steering wheel.

Every evening that week Cole took Lindsey out to dinner, introducing her to one after another of his favourite restaurants. They dined on Chinese food beside the Main River, ate high over Frankfurt in a revolving restaurant above a brewery, and gorged on pizza at a small Italian *gasthaus*.

On each occasion, Lindsey discovered more to admire about Cole. He was intelligent and witty, with strong convictions about his life and his work. Billy was constantly singing his praises, stressing his enormous dedication to duty. Lindsey found herself looking forward to seeing Cole with increasing anticipation as the days passed. The only shadow cast was his flying. Pushing it to the back of her mind, she refused to think about it.

On Friday evening Cole drove her to a little town near the air base where he stopped across the street from a small, modern building. Lindsey admired the neat houses, a few of which sported window boxes brimming with primroses in gay spring colours. 'We haven't been here before, have we?' she asked him. 'This town looks so different from the others we've driven through. The streets are wider, and the houses look almost like any suburb in America.'

'That's because Zeppelinheim is a comparatively new town,' Cole told her. 'It was built to house the people who worked on the airships. I thought you might be interested in seeing the museum.'

Inside the building, he led her to several small rooms crowded with tables and glass display cases. An elderly gentleman sitting in a chair, stood up with a broad smile as he recognised Cole. After chatting for several minutes, Cole explained that the man was a former crew member on the Zeppelins, who now worked as a volunteer in the little museum.

Lindsey was amazed at the degree of luxury that had existed on the passenger airships as evidenced by photos and the displays of dishes and linens. The caretaker eagerly followed the two of them around, pointing out items of special interest, while Cole translated his words for Lindsey. Lindsey was not surprised by Cole's willingness to listen to the older man's reminiscences. From her first encounter with Cole, she had been aware of his sensitivity towards others' feelings. Spurred on by Cole's genuine interest, the caretaker became even more expansive, and the talk more technical. Without a qualm, Lindsey abandoned the two men to wander about the rooms on her own, stopping at any display that caught her eye.

Her knowledge of the giant airships was very limited, and therefore she was totally unprepared when she stopped in front of the case devoted to the history and artefacts of the ill-fated Hindenburg. She stared in shock at the photograph of the enormous flames engulfing the giant airship as passengers jumped and fell to the ground, some on fire. Horrified, she read the account of the disaster and of the thirty-six people who died. As she stood paralysed in front of the tragic picture and the charred mementos, the memories of her father's fiery accident flooded over her. Tearing herself from the graphic display case, she walked blindly from the room, fighting incipient tears.

Cole caught her before she reached the street. 'What's wrong, Lindsey? Did you think I'd abandoned you?'

His arms were a welcoming sanctuary, and Lindsey burrowed deep, seeking comfort from his strength and warmth. She muttered weakly into his jacket. 'I'm sorry. It was that picture.' The black cloud of smoke from her father's plane rose before her. She shook her head, trying to dispel the images imprinted on her brain.

He pushed her gently away from him. Tipping up her chin, he waited until she looked at him. 'What picture?'

A tremor shook Lindsey's body. 'Of the Hindenburg burning. It reminded me of my . . . my dad.'

Cole squinted down at her in concern. 'Bill told me about your father's accident.' He paused, before adding, 'Have you ever considered counselling?'

Leaning back, Lindsey frowned in uncertainty up at him. 'What kind of counselling?'

'Have you ever talked to a psychiatrist?'

She shrugged loose from his arms. 'Are you saying I'm crazy?' she asked sharply.

He pulled her back into his arms. 'You don't have to be crazy to go talk to a professional about a problem.'

'What makes you think I have a problem?'

'Remember me? I'm the guy who sat next to you on the plane and saw how terrified you were.'

'Which does not give you the right to tell me how to

lead my life!'

'There's no stigma attached to having fears and needing help to learn how to deal with them,' said Cole gently.

'Since when did you become an authority on psychology, Cole Farrell?' asked Lindsay furiously.

Cole gave her a little shake. 'I don't have to be an authority to see that you'd be happier if you were better equipped to handle your fears.'

Lindsey glared at him defiantly. 'Lots of people are afraid to fly.'

'But I don't care about those other people. I do care about you.'

'Well, who asked you to?' Near tears at Cole's unexpected remarks, Lindsey only wanted to go home. Cole had been so kind and understanding on the plane; why did he have to criticise her now? She turned away from him.

Cole sighed. 'I don't want to fight about this,' he said finally.

Unwilling to accept his reluctant peace offering, she jerked away from him and walked over to the car. 'Take me home,' she ordered.

Cole raised his brows in exasperation, but unlocked the car doors, and helped her in.

Lindsey quickly realised that they were not on the road back to the base. 'I said I wanted to go home.'

'You'll feel better once you've eaten.'

'Of all the patronising remarks!' she exploded. 'Are you going to take me home or not?'

Cole pulled over to the side of the road. Switching off the ignition, he turned to face her. 'No.'

'No?' she screeched. 'What do you mean, no?'

'You asked if I was going to take you home. I was just answering your question.'

Cole's outrageous answer appealed to Lindsey's sense of humour, and in spite of resolving otherwise, she could feel an imp of mirth bubbling up in her. 'Why not?' she demanded, determined not to let him know that she was softening.

'Because I like being with you.' He reached over and wrapped a curl around his fist, tugging her face close to his.

Lindsey resisted only a minute before lifting her lips to his. Several soft kisses were pressed against her mouth, then she obediently parted her lips in response to the increasing pressure of his. The warm, moist tip of his tongue explored the soft recesses of her mouth, and she shivered slightly, aroused by his intimate touch. Cole's hands on her hips sought to mould her body tight against his.

Immediately Lindsey felt a sharp pain in her knee. She jumped as if she'd been shot. 'Ouch!' Rubbing the tender spot, she had to laugh at the expressions of surprise and chagrin which flitted across Cole's face.

He smiled ruefully. 'I guess the front seat of a sports car isn't the best setting for making love.'

Blushing at his words, Lindsey completely agreed. 'I think the successful bachelor needs an automatic shift,' she teased, looking at the offending gear stick with significant meaning.

He started up his car. 'If I can't feed one appetite, I guess I'll have to take care of another.'

Nothing more was said about Lindsey going home, but even as she enjoyed her dinner with Cole, she failed to completely squelch her feeling of resentment over his earlier remarks. What right did he have to psychoanalyse her? Cole's parents were still living; he couldn't possibly understand how little things could trigger a rush of grief over her father's death. As for being afraid to fly, it was a common phobia. He needn't act as if she were some kind of weirdo because of it.

# CHAPTER THREE

DURING the next couple of weeks, life for Lindsey was a mad whirl of helping Helen, playing with her niece and nephews and seeing Germany under Cole's guidance. If a little voice now and then warned her to watch her step, she ignored it. Cole was entertaining and informative, and her visit was certainly enriched by his companionship. Of course there was nothing serious between the two of them. They were just good friends. If sometimes Cole's kisses seemed a little too passionate and her kisses were a too responsive—well, she could always chalk it up to chemistry. Heaven knows they turned into a pretty combustible combination at times. She couldn't deny that she was attracted to Cole, and under different circumstances . . .

But there was no denying the fact of his job. Cole was a pilot, and Lindsey had no intention of ever becoming seriously involved with a man who flew. She had been crushed by the death of one such man, her father; she wasn't about to tempt fate by falling in love with another aviator. Lindsey had a secure future all mapped out for herself, and there was no room in it for Cole.

Of course it was regrettable. There were times, when Cole was wrestling on the floor with Billy's boys, or when he smiled at her, his blue eyes warm with affection, or he was teasing her, face solemn and eyes sparkling with betraying laughter, when Lindsey felt a shaft of pain that soon she'd be leaving Germany never to see him again.

The hardest times might have been when she was in his arms, but for Cole himself. For it was Cole who managed to keep the lid on their passions, Cole who drew back before it was too late and took her home, and besides—Lindsey couldn't control the tiny imp of dissatisfaction that popped up now and again—Cole seemed perfectly content with the present situation. He never whispered words of love, and in fact, was perfectly capable of whispering some outrageously ridiculous comment just when Lindsey was about to lose every vestige of control in his arms. No, there was no doubt that he was enjoying the romance the same way that she was: less than an affair, but a very enjoyable interlude. She should be thankful that he felt that way. There would be no regrets, no guilt feelings when she went home. Yes, she should feel grateful—shouldn't she?

Lindsey asked herself that question once more as she dressed for the party. It was natural to feel let down when something pleasant was drawing to a close, she reminded herself. Tonight was not the night to become depressed about the future; she and Cole were going to a squadron party at the Officers' Club. When Helen had first mentioned the party in Cole's presence, it had seemed to Lindsey that Cole was somewhat reluctant to go, but he had agreed readily enough that she would enjoy it, and so now she was dressing in preparation.

The party was formal, and Lindsey was thankful that Helen had suggested that she pack at least one dressy outfit. While not exactly formal, the teal-blue cocktail pants and top would fit right in, Helen had assured her. Lindsey twisted her body to better study her image in the mirror. The trousers were plain, fitting snugly around her ankles. It was the top which drew the eye, however. One of Lindsey's own creations, the simple batwinged overblouse was the background for a flight of butterflies that she had appliquéd and embroidered in various shades of peach and apricot with blue and turquoise accents. The

simple lines flattered Lindsey's short, slender height,
while the rich colours complemented her golden blonde
hair and brought out deep green highlights in her eyes. A
dusting of powder served to tone down her freckles, if not
completely hide them. Inserting large golden hoops in
her ears, she wrinkled her nose at her reflection. Nothing
for Cole to be ashamed of. Speaking of Cole, she could
hear him talking with Billy, and grabbing up her bag, she
headed for the living room.

The sight of the two men in the living room stopped
her cold. When Helen had said that the party was formal,
Lindsey hadn't stopped to think what Cole would wear.
Accustomed to seeing him in his flight suit or leisure
clothes, she thought he seemed strangely remote in his
dress uniform. The trim blue jacket, nipped in at the
waist, emphasised his military bearing and rugged good
looks, while a medley of brightly coloured medals on one
chest attested to his success in his job. 'Well,' said
Lindsay weakly, stricken by a sudden tightness of breath
combined with a warm sensation in her inner regions,
'you look—er—nice.'

Cole grinned, transforming him from an elegant
stranger to familiar friend. 'Then that makes two of us,
because you look— er—nice, too,' he mimicked wickedly, his eyes glinting warmly as he surveyed her from head
to toe. 'Very nice, indeed,' he added.

Lindsey blushed at his frank appraisal. 'I'm ready,' she
announced unnecessarily.

Helping Lindsey into his car as if she were a precious
gem, Cole complimented her on her outfit and asked if
she'd made it. That set the tone of conversation for the
short drive to the club, but somehow, casual as it was,
Lindsey was aware of undertones that she couldn't quite
decipher. She recalled her impression that Cole had been
reluctant to attend this party. Had Helen taken too much

for granted when she had assumed that Cole was going to invite Lindsey to go with him? Perhaps he had felt obliged to take her under those circumstances. She wished she knew how to ask him without embarrassing them both.

'There's a bar set up over in the corner. Why don't you sit down and save these two seats here for us while I go get us something to drink. Unless you'd rather go with me?' Cole added as he guided Lindsey over to an empty table inside the club's ballroom.

Lindsey looked over at the mob of males surrounding the bar and quickly assured Cole that she'd rather wait. Confirming that she wanted only a glass of wine, he joined the milling mass, where back slaps and friendly grins quickly welcomed him.

'Hi. I don't think I've seen you around here before.' Looming over her was a face that was all nose and freckles. Flashing a lopsided smile, the man added, 'I'm Kelly O'Brien, and this crazy Italian leering at you from behind my back is Tony Vanetti.' The swarthy man behind the speaker smiled shyly at Lindsey. Both men took her answering smile as an invitation to sit, and quickly did so, the first gentleman straddling his chair, his arms resting on its back. Making no effort to hide his interest in Lindsey, he studied her from head to toe.

Diverted by his audacity, Lindsey quirked an amused brow at him. 'Will I pass?'

Raising a blissful face skyward, Kelly spoke dramatically in an exultant voice. 'Ah, a heavenly voice to match the face of an angel! Now, if I just knew her name, I could die happy.'

The long-suffering look on Tony's face told Lindsey that Kelly was an old pro at handing a line to any passable female. What was more, his manner implied that no girl was to take him seriously. Willing to play his game until Cole returned, Lindsey introduced herself.

'Lindsey Keegan? Funny that we haven't heard Cole mention you before. You did come in with Cole Farrell, didn't you?' At her nod, he continued, 'That's really strange.'

'What's strange about Cole bringing me here tonight?'

'Having seen you, nothing. It's just that Cole has supposedly been very attentive lately to the CO's sister. I wonder what happened to her,' he mused, half to himself.

Instantly Lindsey realised that the difference in surnames had led the man astray in his reasoning. Before she could set him straight, however, he continued on:

'I can't say that I blame him, dumping a frump like that when a dish like you came along.'

'A frump?' Lindsey enquired blandly.

'We don't know she's a frump,' interjected Tony in a soft voice.

'We don't have to know it. What else could she be with Jeffries so eager to set her up with dates, and Cole letting on that he was only taking her out to keep the Colonel happy? You only have to look at Jeffries to see that any sister of his is not exactly Cole's type.'

'Why is that?'

'Don't get me wrong, the Colonel is an okay guy, but he isn't exactly a movie star. He's tall and skinny, wears glasses. He wasn't finding the guys down at the squadron standing in line to take out any sister of his. Yes sir, I figure Cole got Jeffries out of a hole.'

Lindsey began to understand Cole's reluctance to bring her this evening. He'd only been taking her out to keep her brother, his boss, happy. That explained why he'd been uncomfortable in the car. He probably didn't want to be seen in public with her. Now that she thought about it, it was a little strange that everything they had done had been with Billy and Helen or just her and Cole.

No wonder he had had no trouble controlling any passion as far as she was concerned. He was probably terrified that she might take him seriously.

'Doing his commander a favour, you think?' she asked, anger smouldering behind her smiling mask.

'She sews for a living,' Tony said in an apologetic tone. He added hastily, 'Cole did say she had a great personality.'

'Great personality,' said Kelly disgustedly. 'That's what you say when the woman is as ugly as sin. He may as well have said she was nice.' Kelly looked beyond Lindsey. 'Cole, we were just talking about you.'

'To my detriment, no doubt,' said Cole drily, putting two glasses down on the table.

'Heck no, Cole, we're your friends,' Kelly hastily assured him. 'We were just telling Lindsey here how smart you are.'

'Oh?' He turned questioning eyes towards her.

'That's right,' she answered sweetly. 'Kelly thought that it was very clever of you to get rid of your commander's sister, an obvious "frump" whom you've been escorting around in order to curry favour with your boss.' She lifted her chin in challenge.

'Thanks, guys. With friends like you, a man has no need for enemies. Let me introduce you to Lindsey Keegan.' Overriding Kelly's assertions that they had already met, he added in measured tones, 'Lindsey is Colonel Jeffries's stepsister.'

'Oops!' Kelly cowered down behind the back of his chair in mock fear. 'Blew that one, didn't we? Sorry, Cole!'

'Come on, Kelly. Think you've done enough damage around here for now, let's mosey on over to the bar.' Tony literally hauled his protesting friend away.

'I suppose that an explanation is in order.' Sensing her

mood, Cole smiled tentatively at her.

'Not at all. I should imagine that escorting the commander's sister is all in a day's work to you.'

'Damn it, Lindsey, you know that's not true! I don't give a hang about whose sister you are. This has nothing to do with Bill.'

'And I suppose that those two friends of yours just made up what they said?'

The abashed look on Cole's face immediately made nonsense of that statement.

'Don't bother to explain.' Lindsey pushed back her chair. 'I'll relieve you of your duties right now. Billy can take me home.'

Two iron fists on her shoulders held her immobile. 'You're not going anywhere until we thrash this out.'

'I'm not interested in anything that you have to say.'

'Liar,' he said softly. 'If you didn't care, you wouldn't be so annoyed.'

'If, by care, you're hinting that I have any personal interest in you, you couldn't be more wrong. It's just that a person wants to be liked for herself, not for . . . for her relatives,' she burst out.

'Use your head for something besides a beautiful ornament, Lindsey,' he said in disgust. 'If those guys down at the squadron had realised what a beauty you are, there'd have been a mob scene at the Jeffries's house. I was just trying to consolidate my position before the other fellows got wind of the truth. Besides,' he added, a grin flickering across his face, 'Bill is the one who steered everyone in the wrong direction.'

'I don't believe you.'

'You should,' he retorted. 'Ask your brother to describe you some time. I would never have recognised you from his description. My guess is he didn't want to sound like he was bragging so he was very low key. "My sister—er—well, she's kind of short, has freckles, and—er—is real nice." ' Wickedly he aped Billy's voice.

In spite of herself, Lindsey was forced to laugh. 'He didn't?' she asked in horror.

'I solemnly swear,' intoned Cole.

'You can't deny that you didn't want to come tonight,' she parried.

'Was I that obvious?' At her nod, he grimaced. 'Sorry. The truth is, I wanted to keep you hidden.'

'Kelly intimated that you agreed with every word Billy said,' said Lindsey coolly, trying to hide her hurt at his words. He really was ashamed of her.

'I cannot tell a lie.' Cole solemnly placed his hand over his heart. 'I did agree with every word your brother said. Because it's true.' Ignoring her indignant gasp, he went on, 'You are short, you are nice, and,' he traced a line on her face with his finger, 'you do have freckles.'

'Beast! You didn't have to add that I had a great personality!' Lindsey discovered that her mood had inexplicably lightened.

Cole's eyes crinkled at the corners with laughter. 'What did you want me to say? That you were a sexy blonde with green eyes that mirror your every mood? That you may be short but you have great legs?'

'Yes.' Her eyes peeped up at him from beneath lowered lashes, before she added demurely, 'You might have added that I can sew.'

'Oh no,' groaned Cole. 'They even told you that?' At her nod, he confessed, 'That was the last nail in the coffin. I couldn't have *paid* any one of those guys to come over to the Colonel's house after that.' He smiled down into her face. 'Forgiven?'

Ducking from the intent look on his face, she picked up her wine glass and took a sip, her 'yes' a slight whisper.

Smart enough not to rush his fences, Cole stood up. 'Let's dance.'

Aware that they were the focus of all eyes, Lindsey held herself stiff in Cole's arms.

'Relax. I'm not that bad a dancer, am I?'

'You know it's not that. I just feel like everyone is staring at me.'

'That's your fault for looking so beautiful tonight. If you didn't want people to stare, you should have worn something else.'

'Like the spaghetti-stained apron I had on the first night you showed up at Billy's?'

Laughing lightly, Cole swung her in a twirl that left her breathless. 'Somehow I think that might make everyone stare too.'

The lilt in his voice, combined with the disturbing light in his eyes, made her even more breathless than the dance movements. 'You could have spread the word that I can't cook. That would have scared everyone away.'

'Not on your life! None of these bachelors watching you with hungry eyes could care less about your cooking skills.' He pulled her tighter against his chest. 'They haven't discouraged me one whit.'

The slow beat of the music pulsated in Lindsey's ears. The spicy scent of Cole's aftershave mingled with the heavy aroma of her own perfume. Somehow her cheek had come to rest against his broad chest. She lifted her head, and stared up into his face, searching for meaning deeper than the light-hearted banter they'd been engaging in. Slowing his steps, but still swaying to the music, he dipped his head and sought her lips—lips she freely offered. His mouth was smooth and firm, and tasted of wine. Her own parted, giving him the access he gently sought. The music, the other couples, all faded away until he was conscious only of Cole and how good he felt pressed against the length of her body. Butterflies in her stomach took wing. She was light-headed—could one glass of wine go to her head like that?

Cole broke off contact and gently pulled her arms down from his shoulders. Tucking her against his side, he started from the dance floor.

Still overwhelmed by the emotions generated by the kiss, Lindsey stared up at him. 'Cole?' All her uncertainties surfaced in the saying of his name.

'The music stopped,' he hoarsely answered one of her unspoken questions, his voice vibrant with feeling.

'Oh!' She looked around in embarrassment. Was it her imagination, or were the other party-goers avoiding her gaze?

Satisfaction shone in Cole's eyes. 'Yes, they saw.'

'You needn't sound so happy about it! I've never behaved like that on a dance floor before.'

Cole grinned. 'Now, that does make me happy!'

'I think that I detect a little masculine preening in that statement,' said Lindsey crossly.

'Without a doubt,' he conceded. 'I was concerned about competition from the other guys, but I think that kiss you just gave me will settle their hash once and for all.'

'Cole! Is that why you kissed me? Just to post a "No Trespassing" sign?'

He smiled lazily at her outburst. 'I want everyone to know that you belong to me. Any objections?'

'I . . . I don't know. I hadn't thought about it.'

'Think about it now. Meanwhile, Bill's been giving us the high sign for several minutes now. I think he wants to introduce you to some people.'

The remainder of the evening passed in a blur for Lindsey. Cole had introduced a new and serious note into their relationship, and she wasn't sure how she felt about that. Attractive and charming, Cole was every woman's dream. He was great fun to be with, witty and entertaining. When they were together, conversation never lagged, and she had found herself confiding to him hopes and dreams she had never before divulged to anyone. In turn, he'd spoken of his aspirations for the future, and it was here that their relationship hit a snag. Never for a minute could Lindsey forget what it was that Cole did for a living. He flew a plane. Just like her father.

Dating him, she had been fairly successful in pushing to the back of her mind the idea that he was sometimes flying when he wasn't with her. She'd been very careful not to ask what he'd done that day, or what he'd planned for the next. There were times it was inevitable that she knew he was airborne because he would tell her he would be away, but most of the time she was able to maintain ignorance. As a wife, it would be impossible for her to ignore what Cole did.

She wondered if Cole's profession were as much an obstacle to their marriage as she thought. Even if she had tried to ignore it these past few weeks, there was no escaping the fact that she knew what Cole was doing. And besides, even if Billy were only her stepbrother, she had managed to reconcile herself to the fact of his flying career. Couldn't she do the same with Cole? Other wives seemed to cope with flying husbands. Helen was the supreme example. Surely a woman didn't go and have four children if she was expecting to have to raise them all by herself. Helen didn't seem to spend every moment considering that her whole life could come crashing down around her at any minute. And certainly she couldn't kiss Billy goodbye so casually before a flight if she were worried that he might not come home again. Many women lived with men in dangerous occupations and grew so oblivious to the dangers involved that it was almost as if they were married to schoolteachers or lawyers. If other women could do it, why couldn't Lindsey?

It was a relief when Cole finally dropped her off at Billy's house after the party. All her self-questioning and doubts had gained her nothing more than an excruciating headache. It was typical of Cole that he recognised her inner turmoil and had not alluded again to the question that he had subtly raised to her. Lindsey was thankful to have the hint of his intentions without him directly posing the question and thereby requiring her to give him an immediate answer.

As she tossed and turned in bed, she knew that in listing the pros and cons of a relationship with Cole, she was deliberately ignoring the most important question of all. Did she love Cole? Surely, if she did, she could overcome her fears. And really, when one considered it, she had coped awfully well with her fears while dating Cole. By the same token, maybe that was an indication that she really didn't care enough about Cole to be concerned.

So much for thinking that Cole had no serious intentions. He might not have mentioned marriage, but there was no question that he had the subject on his mind. Had she missed earlier, more subtle allusions? Life had seemed so much less confusing when she had thought that she and Cole were just having fun, with no serious intentions complicating their relationship. What a mess! Why did Helen have to go and have twins? If Lindsey had stayed in Colorado, she would never have met Cole, and her life wouldn't have been completely turned around by a pair of deep blue eyes. She pounded her pillow in frustration. Maybe she didn't love him after all. Maybe this awareness, this feeling of being more alive when he was around was nothing more than infatuation. If only he didn't fly!

A sleepless night produced no ready answers. Helping Helen, playing with the boys in the park, bathing the babies—all these were automatically performed while Lindsey's mind grappled with her problem. Cole knew of her fear of flying and about her father's fatal accident with its lasting impact on her. Although he had been gentle and patient with her fears, she doubted that he would understand her misgivings about a future that held the possibility of tragedy. How did one go about telling a man that you didn't want to love him for fear that some day you might lose him?

She had always thought that she wanted, had to have, a future that was secure. Not for her would be the anguish and despair that her mother had suffered. On the other hand, while the pain of her father's death and the misery at her inability to comfort her mother were memories that would be for ever with her, wasn't she adult enough to cope with her memories, relegate them to the past where they belonged? Cole could be her future. Didn't she care enough? Why wasn't love easier?

'I think you've been here too long still to be suffering from jet lag, so it must have been the party that wore you out.'

'What?' Jerked from her reverie, Lindsey looked up to see Helen standing in the doorway, a baby in each arm.

Her sister-in-law grinned knowingly. 'You've just about rubbed the finish off that table-top.'

'Oh.'

'Never mind,' Helen laughed. 'The dusting can wait. Sit down and let's talk.'

'About what?' asked Lindsey warily, as she took Matt, already drowsy from his feeding, and sat down in an easy chair.

'Nothing much. Just gossip about the party last night.'

Helen snuggled into a corner of the sofa, the second twin nestled cosily in her arms. 'Did you enjoy yourself?'

'Everyone was very kind.'

'Kind! Curious is what you mean. Cole couldn't have made his intentions more obvious last night if he'd put up a billboard.' When Lindsey failed to answer, Helen asked softly, 'Am I speaking out of turn?'

Lindsey managed a twisted smile before asking a question of her own. 'Helen, does it bother you, what Billy does for a living? I mean . . . well, I was wondering . . . you don't seem to worry . . . well, after all,' she finished in a rush of words, 'Billy does fly a plane, and planes do crash.'

'Billy told me about what happened to your father.' Helen paused. 'I suppose it's only natural that you would worry about that, but truthfully, I seldom think about it. Billy is a very good pilot, well trained. There are rigid training programmes, stringent safety standards, and operational codes that must be met. Oh, I know there are still accidents,' she added, forestalling Lindsey's comment, 'but Billy is probably in much more danger when he gets out on the *autobahn* than he is in the sky. People just hear more about plane accidents because they're so much more dramatic. So to answer your question, no, it doesn't bother me. Besides, Billy's job is important to him; he takes pride in his work, and he believes in what he does.' She looked directly at Lindsey. 'Have you talked this over with Cole?'

'No. He hasn't asked me to marry him; oh, maybe he hinted last night, but I was evasive. I can't let him ask me until I know how I'm going to answer him.'

'Do you love him?'

'I don't know. I keep asking myself that very question. I like Cole and we have great times together. If I loved him, wouldn't I be ready to marry him no matter what?

Instead, I'm getting all hung up on one silly little obstacle.'

'I don't think your fears are silly or little,' said Helen gently. 'I used to think that love conquers all, but I'm not that naïve now. Not everybody falls in love the same way. Who can define love anyway? Poets and writers have tried for years, but I don't think anyone has really succeeded. A person just knows.'

'Well, I don't know,' snapped Lindsey crossly. 'Does that mean I don't love Cole?' She frowned fiercely. 'Cole deserves a wife who loves him wholeheartedly, who can support him in all that he does. How happy do you think he would be with a wife who was terrified every time he stepped out of the door for fear he'd never come back? But, on the other hand, when I think about going home and never seeing him again, I . . . well, I almost panic inside at the thought. Darn these nagging fears! If and when Cole pops the question, I think that I want to say yes, but—I just don't know. It wouldn't be fair to Cole to saddle him with a wife who was riddled with anxiety over his job.'

'I can't tell you how to live your life,' said Helen slowly. 'I know how real these fears are to you. But you two seem so right together. I hate to see your past wipe out your future. I really think that you owe it to Cole to discuss your feelings with him. He's made his intentions pretty clear, and it doesn't appear to me that you've made any attempt to discourage him. Besides, you say that it's not fair to Cole. It seems to me that you're not being fair in making his decision for him. Isn't it up to him to decide what kind of wife he wants?'

'You may be right,' Lindsey conceded. 'Cole is out of town now. He left this morning for Lajes, but he'll be back in a couple of days. I'll tell him then how I feel.'

Helen eyed her curiously. 'How do you feel now?'

'I just got through telling you!'

'No, I mean about Cole being gone. After all, he's not on a boat. He's in a plane.'

She looked at Helen ruefully. 'I try not to think about it. Up until last night I thought I could get away with ignoring it because I didn't think Cole's job was that important to me. If I were his wife, it would be. I don't know. Can I put my past behind me and cope with the idea of a husband who flies? Do I care enough for him to want to try?' she asked darkly.

'I'm afraid those are answers you're going to have to work out for yourself,' Helen said, her eyes troubled at her inability to help Lindsey with her problems.

'Of course they are, but you're an angel for listening to me,' said Lindsey warmly. 'It's a help to talk it over with someone who can think about the problem more objectively than I can. I'll tell Cole what the situation is and that I need more time to discover my own feelings. What's more,' she added as she looked down at the sleeping twin in her arm, 'I think our conversation was so boring that it put these two right to sleep. Think that we can get them into their cribs without waking them up?'

Helen smiled fondly down on Mandy. 'I don't think a bomb could wake this one up.' As she finished speaking the front door opened and Billy walked in. 'Billy! What in the world are you doing home this time of day?' At the serious look on his face, she shrank back into her chair. 'What is it? What's wrong?'

Passing his wife's chair, Billy gripped her shoulder, but it was to Lindsey's side that he went. 'I can only stay a minute, but I wanted to come home and tell you myself before you heard through the rumour mill.'

'It's Cole, isn't it?' Lindsey could barely squeeze the words out through her parched throat.

'Yes. But don't look like that, honey. He's not dead or

anything. It's just that . . . that there's been a little trouble with his plane.'

'What kind of trouble?' asked Lindsey hoarsely.

'There was a bad failure of the turbine section in engine number four. The engine blew, and when it did, it threw some pieces of metal into number three engine, and apparently severed the oil line in number three.'

'Is he going to crash?' Her wild cry awakened Matt, and the baby began to cry. Billy gently rescued his son from her convulsive grip and handed him to Helen, who promptly shushed him.

'Pull yourself together, Lindsey! Going into hysterics isn't going to help Cole.'

'What is? He's going to die, isn't he?'

Ignoring her final question, Billy continued, 'As soon as the incident happened, Cole radioed Air Traffic Control. They alerted Rota Naval Air Station in Spain. Cole was about five hundred miles from the coast when it happened. Rota immediately notified all ships in the area to keep on the lookout.'

'I thought you said he didn't crash.'

'Standard precautions. Cole is still airborne and he has every intention of flying the plane into Rota. Meanwhile, Air Rescue has been launched. Lindsey, Cole is a excellent pilot; if anyone can bring everybody home safe, Cole can.'

'If! What do you mean if?' cried Lindsey hysterically.

'I won't lie to you: this is a full-blown emergency. Cole is flying that plane on the ragged edge of control, and it's possible that they could crash at any minute. They're leaking oil and he's going to have to fly the plane less than fifty feet above water. We have to trust Cole on this one. He's there and we're here. One thing, Lindsey: Cole isn't going to gamble with the lives of his crew and passengers. If he can't bring that bird in safely, he'll ditch at sea.'

'At sea!' Lindsey could barely make out Billy's face through the tears streaming down her own.

'They'll be okay. The plane has lifeboats and the crew is trained. But that's just an extreme possibility now. Cole says he thinks he can make it in to Rota okay.'

'Thinks!' she cried bitterly.

'I have to get back to the squadron. Helen?' Billy looked over at his wife.

'We'll be okay here, Billy. Who else is on the plane?' He rapidly reeled off the list of names and assured her that each wife had been notified and someone had been dispatched to stay with her through the long ordeal of waiting. Then he left as quickly as he had come.

Lindsey sat numbly in the living room all afternoon. She was vaguely aware of action around her as other wives came by and efficiently collected the Jeffries children and bore them away to play with their own offspring. Even the twins were taken to a neighbour's. Lindsey was grateful that no one wanted to talk to her or discuss what was happening. Several times Helen went to the phone and talked in hushed tones, but each time she came away shaking her head to indicate no further news. Once she informed Lindsey that Cole was nearing Rota and that all available fire trucks and ambulances were waiting near the runway for him. Instead of reassuring Lindsey, the news convinced her that a crash was inevitable.

Desperately she tried to block out recurring memories from her past. The noise and smoke of her father's fiery crash. Her mother sobbing for hours, night after night, the lonely sound terrifying to the small child in the next room. A table laden with salads, cakes and casseroles. The guilt she'd felt when she had enjoyed a piece of chocolate cake and then later seen her mother surreptitiously empty her own plate down the waste disposal. Lindsey's friends who didn't know what to say and wanted to be out playing instead of sitting quiet in a house of mourning. The sight of her mother's face at the funeral, pale and drawn with eyes deep-set within smudged holes. The tearful farewells. And worst of all, the fear that seemed to ooze from her mother, sensed by the small child as a dog smells out fear. Gradually the fear subsided, and the crying grew less. Caroline had talked about Lindsey's father with her, and the two of them had laughed and cried over fond and silly memories. The wounds healed, but the scars remained. Lindsey would never ever forget the sound of her mother's tears in the night or the fear.

Her own tears had long ago dried up and her body was drained of all emotion when Billy finally came home. The intense look of joy on his haggard face told the whole story before he even spoke. Rushing over to Lindsey, he pulled her out of the chair and swung her around the room. 'Cole said to give you this,' and he planted a big kiss on Lindsey's cheek.

'He's okay? You're sure?'

'Talked to him on the phone myself. Said he's exhausted. He had to hold the rudder all the way in to keep the plane flying straight. We're sending some maintenance troops down tonight to look over the plane and see what happened. A C-141 will drop Cole and the rest of the crew off here tomorrow.'

To his bewilderment, Lindsey burst into tears. 'Didn't you hear what I said, honey? Cole is okay and sends you his love. There's nothing in that to cry about, is there?'

For answer, Lindsey just buried her head deeper into his shoulder and sobbed louder. As his arms tightened around her, he spoke helplessly over her shoulder, 'Helen?'

'She'll be okay in a minute. Those are tears of relief; the wait was been agonising for her. Here, Lindsey,' Helen handed her a handkerchief. 'You're getting Billy's uniform all wet!'

Sniffing loudly, Lindsey dabbed at the damp spot on Billy's jacket. 'I'm sorry.'

'Hey, kid, don't worry about it. Don't you know that you're worth more to me than an old jacket any day?'

A water-logged smile was the best that Lindsey could muster for her concerned brother and his wife. Excusing herself to them both, she hurried off to her room where she could be alone with the painful truth. Two things had become very clear to her during the long trial of waiting. There was no longer any question about whether she loved Cole. She did—with an intensity and need the very depths of which frightened her. Because along with her discovery of her love, she had realised one other thing. It was impossible for her ever to marry Cole. There was no way that she could ever subject herself to such a agonising nightmare again. Helen had been right: love didn't conquer all.

A restless night failed to weaken Lindsey's resolve. She had only been fooling herself in thinking that she and Cole could ever share a future. Announcing her plans at breakfast had brought forth a stormy response. Billy tried to persuade her that her reasoning was cock-eyed but found her unwilling to listen to any of his arguments, and he had finally slammed out of the door to work, waking up the twins.

Seeing the mutinous look on Lindsey's tear-stained face, Helen had wisely chosen to skirt the issue of Cole and instead concentrated on her own household's activities. In a house occupied by four vociferous youngsters, Lindsey was soon caught up in demands to be fed or watered or changed. If her mind continued to dwell on Cole and their coming interview, and if she were absent-minded and vague, Helen was kind enough to ignore it. Without a word the latter had taken the pink dress off Matt and put it on Mandy, and rescued Billy's blue uniform shirts from going into the washer with some red towels. Undoubtedly, however, she must have been as relieved as Lindsey when Cole had finally shown up at the apartment shortly before lunch.

One look at Cole, wearing weary lines that a smiling face couldn't hide, and Lindsey's resolve almost melted away. She wanted to throw herself into his arms and declare her love here and now. Instead she stood stiffly as he gave her a swift kiss before greeting Helen and the boys. Charlie demanded to be swung high into the air and Paddy, who was old enough to pick up some of the talk by the neighbours, asked Cole if it were true that he was a hero. It twisted Lindsey's heart to see how, anxious as Cole was to get her alone, he patiently satisfied the boy's curiosity. He even took the time to enquire of Helen as to the twins' prowess. Quick tears sprang to her eyes. The woman Cole married would be very lucky.

Emerging from the apartment, they found their progress down the stairs impeded by neighborus, who, hearing their voices, came out to ferret from Cole details of the near-disaster. He waved aside praise of his own skills, giving the credit for their safe arrival in Spain to the entire crew. Some of the men teased Cole about attention-grabbing tactics, and Lindsey was appalled until she realised that the laughter and banter were their way of expressing relief and joy that disaster had been averted. At last, plaudits for Cole's skill and courage ringing in their ears, they managed to reach the outer door and escape.

The day was grey and cloudy, a smell of rain in the air. Cole walked over to his car, but Lindsey stopped him from opening the door. 'Let's go for a walk in the woods. I—we—need to talk.'

Eyeing her in concern, Cole acquiesced. 'Have you your ID so we can get back through the gate?'

At her nod, he took her hand and they headed down the street through the housing area, reaching the gate without further hindrance. Cole briefly greeted the guard as they stepped past, and soon the coolness of the woods embraced them. Moisture began to drip from the sky, and the woods smelled of damp pine. In the distance a woodpecker could be heard drilling a tree, and an insect buzzed nearby. Overhead a plane from Frankfurt's international airport circled to land, the sound reminding Lindsey of the barrier that stood between them. Cole seemed content simply to stroll along holding her hand, and she was reluctant to bring up a subject that would blast to smithereens the peaceful atmosphere around them.

Cole squeezed her hand. 'You said that you wanted to talk,' he reminded her.

It was too soon. She put off the inevitable. 'I'm glad you're safe.' That, at least, was true.

'You don't think I'd let anything happen to me now that I've got you, do you?'

Lindsey closed her eyes in pain. Explaining to Cole wasn't going to be easy.

'I thought that I might see you down at the squadron when I got in, but Bill explained that you weren't up to it.'

'No . . . I . . . Cole . . .' She looked helplessly up at him.

He reached for her, gently framing her face with large, gentle hands. His thumbs softly traced her cheekbones before he dipped his face, to possess her lips. Like a bereft child, Lindsey clung to Cole, her body seeking comfort and reassurance. Her response seemed to release some banked-down emotions of Cole's, and fiercely he pulled her tightly against his firm, muscled body. Her arms clenched around his neck, Lindsey could feel his heart racing and hers pounding as it kept pace. A whirring of bicycle tyres could be heard nearby, and children's voices carried faintly on the breeze, but her entire world was focused on Cole. A new and different Cole. His kisses were hard and demanding, and he forcefully thrust his way into her mouth. In spite of herself, Lindsey found her body becoming soft and yielding, thrilling to his mastery. Here was no gentle kiss of friendship, this was the kiss of the conquering hero, a man who had faced death head-on and won, and now was claiming the warrior's victory kiss. Was this kiss Cole's way of saying how glad he was to be alive? Suddenly she wondered if he had been afraid. Panting slightly, she drew back.

Cole considered her question, an intense frown on his face. 'Only a fool wouldn't have been scared in that kind of situation. The danger isn't in being afraid; it's in allowing fear to take over and render you incapable of thinking out your situation. Of course I was scared. We were all scared.' A rough thumb caressed her throbbing lips. 'It was worth a little fear for a welcome home like this. I want to know that this kind of homecoming is always waiting for me. Marry me?' The casualness of the question was belied by the intent look in his eyes as he made to pull her back into his arms.

She tugged free. 'No.' She could barely push the denial past trembling lips.

He didn't hear her. 'We can go up to Denmark, or would you rather fly home and get married in Colorado with your folks?'

'Cole, I said no. I can't marry you.'

He stepped back, stunned by her reply. 'Why, Lindsey? I thought you and I had something special going for us.'

'I'm sorry, Cole. I . . . I . . . just can't,' she whispered brokenly, turning away from him.

'What kind of damn fool answer is that?'

'You don't understand.'

'Then why don't you explain it to me?'

'It just wouldn't work out.'

His patience visibly wearing thin, Cole jerked her around to face him. 'That's not an explanation!'

She blinked rapidly, trying to keep tears at bay. 'I won't, I can't marry a man who flies.'

'You've waited until now to decide that? What the hell did you think I did for a living? Washed planes?'

'I thought it wouldn't matter—I really did. But it does. Yesterday proved that to me. I'd live a life of terror every time you walked out the door.'

'For heaven's sake, Lindsey, an incident like yesterday is a extremely rare. There's no more danger in what I do than in you driving to your shop.'

'Whether there is or not, isn't the point, Cole. I believe it's dangerous, and I simply can't handle the pressures of your kind of life.'

'You've known from the beginning that I was a pilot. Or didn't you care?' he lashed out. 'Maybe you were just bored and I provided diversion.'

'It wasn't like that.' Lindsey reached out a beseeching hand. 'I thought that we were just friends. I thought that's what you wanted, too. It didn't matter then what you did.'

'Sure,' he groaned. 'A little harmless flirtation was all you had in mind. It probably wasn't part of your plans that I'd wreck everything by being fool enough to fall in love with you.'

A light rain began to fall, the moisture cold and clammy on Lindsey's face. As cold and clammy as her inner self. She thrust her clenched fists deep into her raincoat, her shoulders hunched defensively against his verbal attacks. 'What about me?' she cried. 'Do you think I wanted to fall in love with you? Plans. Yes, I had plans. I planned to fall in love with a man who keeps both feet firmly on the ground at all times. Then you came along and ... and I just couldn't help myself.'

Cole grabbed her by the shoulders and gazed intently down into her rain-washed face. 'You admit that you love me?'

'Of course. Don't you see? If I didn't love you, then your flying wouldn't bother me.' She gave a bitter little smile. 'I wish we'd never met.'

He threw her a quick look from beneath lowered brows. 'Other women's husbands fly.'

'Other women didn't see their father killed before their eyes!'

'I haven't forgotten that. It was a tragic thing to happen to you, but that was over fifteen years ago, and things have changed since then. Flying is safer.'

'Not safe enough for me.'

'I can't believe that you expect me to give you up because of ... of ...' He shook his head like a wounded animal. 'Damn it, Lindsey, I love you!'

She took a deep breath. This was the crucial question. 'Do you, Cole?'

'You know I do. What do I have to do to prove it?'

'Quit flying.' She looked at him steadily as she said it. Her words were a blow to him.

He backed away, slowly shaking his head. 'No, I can't do that. It's my life, Lindsey. Something I've wanted to do ever since I was a kid. I trained for it, I worked hard to get where I am. I'm a good pilot, and the Air Force needs good pilots. If I get out, what else am I trained to do?'

'But that's just it!' she cried eagerly. 'You don't have to get out. I don't care if you stay in the Air Force. Surely you wouldn't have any trouble getting a desk job? Billy would help you, I know he would.'

'It wouldn't work. I don't want to fly a desk. Besides, if I refused to fly any more, I could kiss my career goodbye, and I'd resent your forcing me into it.'

'Then that's it, isn't it? You won't change for me, and I can't accept what you are now.'

'So you're taking the cowards way out?'

'Am I? I suppose to your way of thinking, I am.' Lindsey choked back a sob, staring numbly at the leather patch that spelled out his name on his flight jacket. 'It just wouldn't work, Cole.'

'We can make it work.'

Miserable, she shook her head. 'I'm sorry.'

His grip tightened painfully. 'I never thought I'd be so wrong about anyone. You're the last person that I'd suspect of being a quitter,' he said ruthlessly.

But his angry attempt to ignite her fighting spirit failed. Aware that she had raised false expectations, knowing that he had every cause for his anger, she offered no more excuses. Chilled by Cole's harsh words, she barely felt the cold seeping through her coat and the water running down her neck. The rain was coming down harder now, and her hair was plastered across her face and down her neck in wet tendrils.

A lone rivulet travelled down her nose and dropped to her lips where it clung, attracting Cole's attention. Swearing harshly beneath his breath, he hauled her hard against his muscular chest, thrusting his fingers through her hair and holding her head immobile as he stared fiercely down at her. Salty tears mingled with the rain on her lips, and she could taste both as Cole punished her with a savage kiss that contained all his anger and frustration.

Knowing this would be their last kiss, Lindsey not only refused to fight him, she met him eagerly, her own over-heated emotions glorying in this elemental contact between male and female. Unzipping his bulky jacket, she slid her arms inside and clung to his waist. The cold, the rain, his angry words, all faded in importance against the taste and feel of his mouth. She burrowed closer, wanting to warm herself in the heat that emanated from his body. Breathing deeply of his masculine scent, she offered no resistance to his probing kisses or searching hands.

Cole was the first to pull away, panting heavily. 'Lindsey, this is ridiculous. We're both getting soaked. Say what you will, your actions prove that we want each other, we need each other. Damn it, you can't kiss me like that and then turn around and say this is the end. It isn't fair!'

'You're right,' she said in a conscience-stricken voice. 'I should never have allowed things to get this far.' She paused, then added in a quiet, resolute voice. 'I'll . . . I'll go home with you now and spend the night. If you want.'

'Spend the night?' he repeated explosively. 'The hell you will! And what's that supposed to mean?'

'Just what I said. You said you wanted me . . . that I wasn't being fair to you. So,' she concentrated on his left ear, 'I can't marry you, but maybe I do . . . do owe . . . you something, and . . .'

Cole interrupted her. 'A generous offer indeed,' he pronounced. 'No, thanks. I'll pass on your benevolent offer. I don't want any half-way measures from you. It's all or nothing.'

'All or nothing from me,' she choked. 'I do the giving-in, the compromising, the suffering. And you, Cole, what will you do for me? Give up flying?'

'We've already been over that. You know I can't give it up,' he said tightly.

'And you know that I can't marry you.' She put up a restraining hand as he made to pull her back into his arms. 'No, Cole,' she shook her head wearily. 'Please. Let's just say goodbye now. If you really love me as you say you do, you'll let me go. I can't . . .' Her voice faltered as she turned away.

'Lindsey.' A new and softer note entered his voice. 'Just remember two things. I love you and . . .'

He was silent so long she turned back towards him. 'And?' she prompted in a voice she scarcely recognised as her own.

'If you ever decide to grow up and take a chance on life . . .' the challenge lay still and quiet in the rainwashed day before he added, 'your brother will know where to find me.'

The tears running freely down Lindsey's face were indistinguishable from the falling rain. Her throat was swollen with emotion, rendering her incapable of speech. Hungrily she stared up into his face, wanting to memorise it for all time, but it was a stranger's face she saw. Gone was the warmth in the bright blue eyes, missing was the generous smile, the light of love. In their place was nothing more than a marble statue. Involuntarily Lindsey reached up and caressed the still, cold cheek of the man she'd grown to love over the past few weeks. 'Goodbye, Cole,' she whispered brokenly.

Cole imprisoned her shaking hand in his larger one, squeezing it painfully before he turned it over and lingeringly pressed a firm kiss on her palm. Electricity ran up her arm at the touch of his lips and she almost cried out. Slowly Cole curled her fingers over her palm, capturing the kiss. 'Not goodbye,' he corrected. *'Auf*

*Wiedersehen.'*

A stiff salute and he was gone, striding deep into the woods. Lindsey watched him until the falling rain and tall, misty trees hid him from her view. A sharp pain pierced her chest, and unconsciously she cupped her hands together and held them both tightly to her mouth, her lips seeking the spot touched by Cole's, as if by doing so, she could feel his lips on hers. The rain increased in velocity, pounding down in hard, angry sheets.

# CHAPTER FOUR

WITH a loud rush of wings, several magpies scattered into the air, their long black tails iridescent against the blue sky. Lindsey smiled as she recalled Billy telling her that, although the falcon was the official Academy mascot, magpies populated the Academy grounds in such large numbers that the cadets dubbed them terrazzo falcons.

They could have the place as far as she was concerned. She wouldn't be here now if it weren't for a client. She had been commissioned to design and execute a quilt for a retired Air Force general, a surprise present from his wife. Since the couple now resided in Colorado Springs, the woman had been adamant that some symbols from the Air Force Academy be included in the design.

Coming out here today had almost required more courage than Lindsey was capable of mustering. Every man in blue that she saw twisted the knife of pain deeper in her heart. Near her two young girls spoke to a passing cadet. The young man paused courteously, then pointed off in the distance. Moving briskly on, he seemed unaware of the wistful admiration on two female faces watching him disappear down the ramp. Lindsey smiled sadly. Military men always seemed to have the edge when it came to attracting women. Maybe it was the uniform, maybe it was the way they held themselves so proud and erect. Maybe it was because they seemed so invincible.

Like the man headed in her direction. Vaguely she approved his military bearing. Tall, walking proud; even

with a hand clutching at his wheel hat to prevent the
small gusts of wind from capturing it, he exuded self-
assurance with his commanding air. A sob caught in her
throat. He looked like Cole. She scolded herself for the
thought; must she try to see him in every man wearing
Air Force blue? She had been home three months now.
Even if she could never completely forget him, surely by
now the pain should have eased, the memories faded.
Cole wasn't the only tall, brown-haired man in blue
uniform. There were lots of broad-shouldered officers,
their firm chests, covered with brightly-coloured rib-
bons, sloping down to slim hips. Even the aviator
sunglasses were worn by many men, not just pilots. Just
because this man walked like Cole, his long, lean legs
eating up the distance between them ... Her breath
caught, stopping her heart between beats. It was Cole.

She couldn't deny the swift rush of happiness that she
felt at seeing him. What on earth was Cole doing here in
Colorado? Was he looking for her? She wanted to turn
and flee, but trembling legs held her rooted to the marble
squares. Cole looked so remote, so implacable. He wasn't
pleased to see her. Tightly clutching the straps of her bag,
she spoke first. 'Cole! What a surprise!' Her voice was
too loud, too high.

He gravely inclined his head. 'Lindsey. It is a surprise.
I never expected to see you anywhere near here; I
thought you stayed as far away from the Air Force as you
could.'

The tone might be mild and the words bland, but
Lindsey immediately grasped the unspoken words that
hovered in the air between them. Cole had gone straight
for the jugular. Even though the sun shone brightly down
on them, Lindsey shivered at the memory of an icily
angry Cole calling her a coward and accusing her of

leading him on. She hadn't—at least, not intentionally. He'd doubted her, but she had loved him. He had insisted that if she had really loved him, she wouldn't allow her fears to keep them apart. But then didn't that go for him too? If he had really loved her, wouldn't he have given up flying for her? Her colour high, she opened her mouth to once again defend her position, only to swallow the words. If Cole really cared for her, he would have been more understanding about her fears. Instead she repeated her first remark. 'What a surprise to see you here.'

'I'm stationed at the Academy now.'

'Here at the Academy?' Lindsey echoed his words, thoughts whirling madly around in her head. Why on earth was Cole here? He had sworn that he wouldn't quit flying for her or anyone else. Could it possibly be that after she had left, he had regretted his hasty words? A quick glance up at his face told her nothing, his feelings concealed behind his sunglasses. At one time she'd known his every thought, his every dream. Now, she could only see herself mirrored in the shiny lenses, her hair blown into curly disarray by the gusty winds that punctuated the warm June day. Freckles stood out like dark brown beacons against her pale skin, evidence of her tangled emotional state.

Once they had had so many things to say to each other that their time together had always been much too short. Now, Lindsey could only stare at Cole, rendered speechless by his unexpected appearance and her own emotional reaction to it. She wondered how Cole felt about seeing her again. The dark glasses were an effective mask, hiding those intense blue eyes that could be warm with tenderness or dancing with laughter. His mouth was hard, unforgiving. She could remember the times when those same firm lips had softened against her own. She knew the feel, the taste of his mouth. Want and need flooded through her body, swamping her with their intensity. She barely restrained trembling fingers from reaching out and tracing the outline of his lips. Then they tightened in exasperation and she realised that he'd been speaking to her. 'Er, what did you say, Cole?'

'I asked how it happens that you're wandering around out here?' He spoke distinctly, as if to a child.

'I'm ... I'm working.' Stumbling over her words, Lindsey briefly explained about the commissioned quilt. 'I've been photographing and sketching different designs and motifs, some of which I'll incorporate into my final design.'

'Then I mustn't keep you. It was nice seeing you again.'

'Er, yes.' Politeness for politeness's sake.

Her eyes swelled with tears as Cole walked away. Would the pain never go away? It didn't seem possible that only four months had passed since their first meeting. How little did she suspect then what a cataclysmic encounter it would turn out to be. Meeting on a plane had turned out to be quite prophetic: a plane had brought them together, and planes had driven them apart. At least when she left Germany, she had thought that he was out of her life for good. What would it mean having him here in Colorado? There was no need for them ever to meet, she told herself. Certainly, he had given no evidence that he wished to renew any old acquaintances. That was fine with her. She had no desire to see Cole again. Did she?

Unfortunately, while the fact that there were insurmountable obstacles to their getting married wiped out any chance of their sharing a future, it hadn't erased the memories of the good times they'd shared. How did one erase a useless love when every rainy day, every butterfly flitting by, every drone of a plane overhead brought back the piercing, sweet memories?

Leaning against the waist-high concrete wall overlooking the terrazzo, Lindsey fought to bring her emotions under control. She still had a few sketches that she wanted to make, and if she allowed her weaknesses to drive her away now, she'd just have to return again. And that she had no intention of doing. The last thing she wanted to risk was another unexpected meeting with Cole.

Looking down over the wall, she spotted the planes that decorated the four corners of the grassy centre. Just looking at them sent shivers up and down her spine. It was okay for men to talk of the glories, to aim for the skies, but what of the women they left below them on the ground? She hated herself for being a coward. Other women thought nothing of marrying a pilot. Throughout the centuries women had sent their husbands and lovers off to war. She thought again of her mother's anguish following her husband's death. No, Lindsey admitted that she lacked the courage to accept Cole and what he had to offer her. She needed stability, security, a man who would come safely home to her each night. Why couldn't he understand that?

Darn! Why did he have to come here now? Just when she was starting to pull herself together, to convince herself that her acquaintance with him had been the equivalent of a shipboard romance, lovely while it lasted but certainly not meant to endure. He had told her that if she changed her mind, all she had to do was let him know. Had he come here in hopes of hearing that absence had made the heart grow fonder? If so, he'd be gratified to know that it had. Not a day passed that she didn't regret her decision. Unfortunately, nothing had made her change it.

She wished she could believe that Cole had changed his mind. Could it be that he was here because he was giving in to her demands? Closing her eyes against the hot summer sun, Lindsey could see Cole standing before her, his whole body stiff with cool disdain. He hadn't forgiven her for what he had called her lack of courage. The firm lips, the resolute jaw . . . She remembered their parting in Germany and the conviction with which he had spoken about his love of flying and his belief that he was needed in the job he'd chosen to do. No, Cole was not the man to give up his dreams and his beliefs because of her fears.

An hour later she sat dejectedly in her car. Her sketches were horrible; inspiration had ceased to flow. How could she copy mosaics, draw the skyline or even pretend to be creative when all she saw before her was Cole's face? She wanted nothing more than to curl up at home and give in to self-pity.

Unfortunately, she had to go by her mother's to drop off a pillow she had promised to bring her this afternoon. Hiding her misery from her mother's sharp eyes was not going to be easy. Caroline had no idea that Lindsey's visit to Germany had been anything other than a wonderful time. Wonderful time, Lindsey thought bleakly. Wonderful times didn't leave you hurting so badly you wondered if you'd ever heal.

Walking to the door of her mother's house, she hoped to make a quick getaway.

'You'll never guess what!' Caroline, Lindsey's mother, met her at the door, her face beaming with pleasure.

'You've won the Colorado lottery,' guessed Lindsey.

'Don't I wish!' retorted Caroline. 'A friend of Billy's is

in town, and I've talked him into coming to dinner.'

It never failed to amaze Lindsey how many of Billy's old schoolmates and service buddies managed to find their way to Billy's old home and Caroline's dinner table. Lindsey realised that Charles missed his son terribly, and that this was Caroline's way of easing his loneliness. A sudden premonition gripped her. 'Tonight?' she asked hoarsely.

'Yes,' Caroline glowed. 'Isn't that wonderful?'

'Great,' lied Lindsay. 'Well, you all have fun. I'm off.'

'Oh no, you don't, young lady. I heard you earlier when you promised Charles to stay and eat with us tonight. He's out fixing your favourite grilled chicken right now.'

'I—er—forgot,' stammered Lindsey, her mind racing, 'I forgot that I have . . . have a date with Ross.'

'Good try. Unfortunately for you I happen to know that Ross is out of town collecting a deposition. He stopped by to see Charles before he left. Why are you suddenly so set on not staying for dinner? Is it because I said I'd invited Major Farrell to dinner?'

'Heavens, no!' She forced a gay, artificial laugh. 'I guess Ross must have forgotten our date, in which case there isn't any reason why I can't stay.' She took a deep breath. There was no sense in putting off the inevitable. 'Actually, I know Major Farrell. I met him in Germany.' Caroline grinned. 'No doubt that's why he was so quick to call Charles and me up. He wanted to see you again.'

Lindsey shook her head. 'He doesn't even like me very much.'

'I see.' Caroline gave her a piercing look. 'Had a spat, did you? I imagine he's a young man with a mind of his own.'

A spat was hardly the appropriate word to describe a parting that had emotionally shredded her, Lindsey thought bleakly. Forcing the words past a gigantic lump in her throat, she denied her mother's conclusions. 'Cole was just someone in Billy's squadron. That's all there is to it.'

'Surely not quite all?' Cole's provocative remark preceded him into the room, Charles following.

'What's this about you knowing Cole?' her stepfather asked, a twinkle in his eye, as he crossed the room to give her a quick hug.

'We met when I went to Germany,' Lindsey repeated, daring Cole to enlarge on her bald statement.

A devilish light gleamed in Cole's eyes as he promptly took up her challenge. 'Bill wanted someone in the squadron to take his little sister around and show her the sights. The guys weren't exactly standing in line to volunteer, but I seen my duty and I done it.'

The audacity of Cole's remark took Lindsey's breath away, remembering how she had accused Cole of that very thing. 'Why, you, you . . .' she spluttered.

Charles's quick laugh boomed through the room. 'I'll bet after everyone seeing Lindsey, the next time Billy needs a volunteer, he'll have more than he knows what to do with!'

Cole coolly surveyed Lindsey over the rim of his glass, before casually agreeing with her stepfather. Making sure that she knew he was only agreeing to be polite, thought Lindsey furiously. Accepting a glass of wine from Charles, she remained aloof from the conversation of the other three. Cole was soon telling anecdotes about Germany and his work. Lindsey noticed that Billy figured in many of Cole's tales, to Charles's visible satisfaction. They all seemed to think what Cole did was so wonderful. Lindsey fidgeted in discomfort. How could they laugh at some of those stories? Just thinking about

Cole's near-disaster still had the power to make her ill. Abruptly she interrupted the conversation. 'Ask Cole about his engine trouble over the ocean.'

As all eyes turned in his direction, Cole shrugged. Describing the incident in terse phrases, he added, 'It was nothing. Lindsey makes too much of it.'

She could feel a warm flush crawl up her throat at the underlying scorn of his remark. 'Everyone could have been killed!' she cried.

'Nobody was,' returned Cole indifferently.

'Lindsey isn't much on flying,' her stepfather apologised for her.

Cole's eyes narrowed to slits as he looked over at Lindsey. 'I know. I'm surprised she made it back to Colorado!'

Charles chuckled. 'That makes two of us. Billy had her sedated to the gills, and she was still a basket case when she arrived back. Scared Caroline half to death.'

'I'm glad you were so amused,' Lindsey snapped, on the brink of tears.

'Now, honey, I was just teasing you,' said Charles in bewilderment. 'You were telling it as a funny story on yourself just the other night.'

'Why don't you come and help me in the kitchen?' Caroline suggested diplomatically to her distraught daughter.

Lindsey followed her mother from the room. How could Charles bring up her weakness in front of Cole? Of course, he didn't know about their past history, but still . . . She wouldn't have cared, had it been anyone else but Cole. She didn't even have to look at him to know that he'd felt nothing but contempt for her at Charles's words. So much for his admiration of her courage in flying over to Germany. He was just like a child, she thought bitterly. When he couldn't have his own way, it was all her fault. He never even considered her feelings. The fear she'd felt about her own plane journey was nothing compared to the terror she had endured when he was in trouble. How like him to belittle it!

'Charles didn't mean to upset you,' Caroline said soothingly.

'I know. It's just that,' Lindsay gestured aimlessly about the kitchen, 'I . . . I would rather he hadn't told Cole.'

'Cole's certainly nice.' Her mother deftly added dressing to the green salad, and tossed the vegetables to coat them well.

Lindsey absently picked up a carrot stick and began to munch. 'And why didn't I mention him when I got home?'

'I expect you forgot,' Caroline said impishly, not believing it for a second. 'How nice that he was able to take you about sightseeing. Of course, with you being his commanding officer's sister, I'm sure it didn't hurt him.'

Lindsey winced to hear her mother echo her own previous conclusions. 'I'm not such an old hag that a man only asks me out because of who I am,' she said diffidently.

'Of course you're not. I didn't really mean to insinuate that you were. Still, if there had been any other motive to Cole's escorting you about, he would have called you when he arrived here, don't you think?' She gave Lindsey a look of innocent inquiry as she opened the oven.

'Perhaps he felt a little awkward calling up someone who had refused to marry him,' retorted Lindsey without thinking. The look of astonishment, quickly replaced by satisfaction, that crossed Caroline's face brought home to Lindsey what her impetuous remark had wrought.

'So,' said her mother triumphantly, 'I knew something had gone on over there. I haven't been your mother for twenty-three-odd years without learning something about you.' She hesitated, before adding, 'Obviously you didn't care to discuss it with me. Do Billy or Helen know?' At Lindsey's nod, Caroline went on briskly, 'Well, when you want to talk about it, I'm ready to listen.'

Lindsey blinked back a tear at her mother's ready sympathy and understanding. 'I can't talk about it now.' She didn't want to bring pain to her mother by reminding her of the death of her first husband; Caroline had suffered enough from that. Picking up the finished salad, she headed for the patio. 'By the way, Mom, you're the greatest.' The closing screen cut off her mother's answer, but not before Lindsey had seen the pleased expression on her face.

She set the salad on the picnic table, uncomfortably aware that Cole's presence was already heightening her senses. As he laughed at a remark of Charles's it took all her restraint to keep from throwing herself in his arms. She wondered what he'd do if she did.

'If you two haven't burned the meat, the rest of the dinner is ready.' At least her voice sounded normal.

'Look who's talking,' Charles immediately riposted. 'This girl of mine is the world's worst cook,' he explained to Cole. 'Don't ever make the mistake of asking her to cook you dinner.'

Cole looked over at Lindsey, cool laughter in the depths of his eyes, and she knew that he was remembering her disastrous spaghetti sauce.

Quickly she changed the subject, blurting out the first thing that came to mind. 'You mentioned earlier that you've been assigned to the Air Force Academy, Cole. How come?'

'New job. I rotated out of Germany after three years, and now I'm going to teach in the military studies department for the next few years.'

Hope almost strangled Lindsey. 'Does that mean that you're no longer a pilot?'

'Not at all.' He looked directly at her. 'It's better for a career profile if one has a little diversity. Plus, the higher-ups here at the Academy like to bring in active-duty officers from all the various fields to give the cadets some role models. That's why I was on the same plane out of Denver as you. I'd been out here interviewing for the job.'

'Won't you miss the flying? To hear Billy talk, pilots have to fly to breathe.' Charles spoke with the fond indulgence of a proud father.

Cole laughed. 'Yes, of course I will, and I'll return to it. But teaching here is an exciting challenge of a different nature. Moulding minds. These young people are the cream of the nation's crop, and our future leaders. Keeping up with them, and dealing with them on a day-to-day basis, will help me hone the leadership skills that I'll need when I go back to flying. These days, being a pilot in the Air Force requires more than proficient flying skills. Of course, those help,' he added with a smile.

As Charles asked him more questions, Lindsey's attention strayed. Charles's special chicken lay un-touched on her plate, the sauce slowly congealing into an unappealing mass. How could she have been so stupid as to hope that Cole had changed his mind? She knew that he was never going to give up flying. Caroline was right; he wasn't interested in her any more. He hadn't made any effort to contact her. She closed her eyes in pain.

'Where are you living, Cole?' Charles's question

diverted Lindsey's attention back to the conversation around her.

'Right now I'm in the VOQ.'

'VOQ?' Lindsey hated herself for being interested enough to ask.

'Visiting Officers' Quarters. But I just closed on a house today.'

'A house? Isn't that quite an enterprise for a bachelor to take on?' Charles asked.

'Sure, but I don't intend to be a bachelor much longer.'

Lindsey looked at him in shock. She wanted to know, but she couldn't ask. Wordlessly she appealed to her mother.

Caroline recognised the silent cry for help, and quickly said, 'That sounds like congratulations are in order. When is the wedding date?'

'It's not. To be perfectly honest, I just decided to get married. I don't have a bride yet.'

Caroline choked on her wine. 'I don't quite understand.'

'It seems to me that in the service when it comes time to select commanding officers and move up the career ladder, the married man has the advantage. So, I decided to get married. Being here in one place for several years, with a job that will give me more free time than I've had in the past, this is the perfect time for me to look around and select a wife.'

'As easy as that?' Lindsey couldn't help the sarcasm that coated her voice. The perfectly awful thought had just struck her that maybe Cole had never loved her. Maybe he'd just wanted to check off another requirement for being promoted.

Cole's cool blue eyes held her own. 'Not quite as easy as all that. There are probably some women around who are afraid to gamble on marrying someone like me.' He added smoothly, as if he hadn't just dealt her a lethal blow, 'I figure, buy a house and get it all fixed up, and the women will just drop into my lap like flies.' He turned to Caroline. 'Unfortunately, now that I've got the house, I really don't know what to do with it. I have a few pieces of furniture that used to be my grandmother's, and odds and ends that I picked up overseas. I sure wish that I knew something about decorating a house.' He paused in speculation. 'I don't suppose you know someone who could help me.'

A foreboding chill held Lindsey motionless in her chair. Don't say it, she silently prayed to her mother.

'Lindsey,' said Caroline decisively. 'With her art background and eye for colour, she's the perfect person to help you out. I haven't the faintest idea how to go about decorating a house, but Lindsey re-did this place for us a couple of years ago. We had planned to hire an interior decorator, but when the woman wanted to throw away Charles's favourite chair and insisted that my mother's marble table didn't match the décor, Charles politely showed her the door. We decided that we'd just have to live with the house the way it was, but Lindsey worked her magic on it, without throwing away anything we loved. We couldn't be happier with the results.'

Cole turned to Lindsey, but before he could say anything, she blurted out: 'I'd love to help you, Cole,'—a lie—'but I'm just swamped with work right now.' She wasn't about to torment herself by helping Cole decorate a house in order to get himself a wife.

Caroline gave her a steady look that told Lindsey that her mother recognised the lie and was disappointed by her daughter's less than gracious behaviour. 'Surely you can take a few hours to help Cole. After all, I understand he acted as your guide to Europe when Billy and Helen were unable to.'

Lindsey bit her lip in chagrin. Caroline couldn't abide bad manners or selfish attitudes. And she was right: she did owe it to Cole to pay him back for his kindnesses. Reluctantly she opened her mouth to acquiesce when it occurred to her that she'd turned Cole down before he'd, even asked her. Maybe he didn't want her any more than she wanted him.

'I wouldn't want Lindsey to neglect her work on my account,' he said virtuously. 'I'll just have to do the best I can.' His pathetic answer, designed to play on Caroline's sympathies, made Lindsey's blood boil.

'I'm sure that Lindsey can fit you in if she tries,' said Caroline firmly. 'Isn't that right, Lindsey?' The angry glint in her eye said it had better be right.

Lindsey knew when she was licked. She might be twenty-three years old, but her mother wasn't above pointing out her duty. Caroline had very rigid standards about repaying obligations, and Lindsey knew that refusing to help Cole would greatly disturb her mother. How long could it take, anyway, to shove around a few pieces of furniture? Surely it wasn't a matter worth upsetting her mother about. 'Yes, of course I'll help Cole,' she agreed grudgingly.

'I appreciate your kind offer,' he said, a tiny quirk appearing momentarily in the corner of his mouth.

Lindsey was furious—at her mother for forcing her hand, and at Cole for seeing her quandary and being amused by it. He knew she didn't want to spend any time with him. Abruptly she pushed back her chair. 'I have to go.'

'So early?' Cole's careless enquiry infuriated her. He couldn't make his lack of interest in her any clearer.

'Tomorrow's my day at the shop,' she said brusquely, kissing her parents goodnight. 'Thanks for dinner. It was delicious, as usual.'

The sardonic lift of Cole's brows told Lindsey he recognised her rush to escape. She raised her chin defiantly. 'Goodbye, Cole.'

His eyes narrowed until only the dark pupils were visible. 'I told you before,' he said evenly, 'not goodbye, *Auf Wiedersehen.*'

As Lindsey opened the back screen door she heard Charles ask, '*Auf Wiedersehen.* What does that mean?'

'It's German. Loosely translated, it means until we see each other again.'

'That's lovely,' Caroline said.

Lindsey slammed the door.


'Well, I don't know,' the middle-aged lady was having trouble making up her mind, 'the doll is charming, but my granddaughter is only three months old.'

'Did you see these darling baby bibs? They're handpainted, but can still go in the washer and drier. And here are some crocheted baby blankets.' Guiding the woman to the babies' corner, Lindsey pointed out quilts, pictures and toys. Thirty minutes later the customer returned to the doll that had first caught her eye. Concluding her purchase, she exited into the late afternoon sunshine.

Thankful that the customer had not left without buying something, Lindsey went into the back for another doll to replace the one she had just sold. In the main shop area the bell over the outside door tinkled as it was opened, and she could hear Sally's voice and a deep, male rumble. Well, Sally could handle the man while she did a little straightening of their stock room. The tourist season was under way, and she and Sally had been rushed off their feet today; as a result, the back room looked like the aftermath of a tornado.

As she worked, her thoughts drifted back to dinner last evening at her mother's house. The shock of Cole's appearance still hadn't receded. Even worse was the knowledge that her love for him had not lessened in their months apart. She had longed to go straight into his arms. Unable to sleep, she had spent the night reminding herself that she could have had that right, if only she'd said the word. That knowledge was of little consolation, because she knew if Cole asked her again to be his wife, she would have to turn him down again. Look how much she had missed him since returning to Colorado. That alone ought to convince her that she couldn't marry him. If she missed him this much after just a short relationship, think what agony life would be if she married him and then he were killed. No, marriage to Cole was not to be thought of. Unfortunately he hadn't lost any of his appeal, she thought wistfully. Caroline and Charles had quickly succumbed to his charm.

And charm he had in abundance. The open-necked shirt he had been wearing had exposed a tanned column of skin that Lindsey had wanted passionately to press her lips against. His eyes seemed bluer and his shoulders broader than she remembered. She had the sense of standing on the edge of a bottomless abyss when she contemplated the time she'd need to spend with him in order to help him with his house. How could her mother do this to her? Perhaps it would have wiser to have explained the situation more clearly to her mother. Caroline would never have pushed so hard if she had realised what pain her actions would cause Lindsey.

If. If she had told her mother, if Cole hadn't come to

Colorado, if Helen hadn't had twins, if Lindsey's father hadn't died. This was stupid. She had to get a grip on herself. It was too late to change the past; she could only hope to cope with the future. Besides, a ray of hope pierced her gloomy thoughts: Cole might have simply agreed with Caroline to avoid any suggestion of discourtesy to his hostess. Now that Lindsey considered the matter, Cole had made no arrangements to get together with her to discuss the matter—she'd been silly to worry. Obviously he had no more desire to see her than she had to see him. She should be happy that Cole had lost all interest in her—very happy. Wiping away a stray tear, she returned to the showroom.

Cole was leaning on the counter, his head thrown back as he laughed heartily at something that Sally had said. Lindsey wondered what Sally's husband would think if he could see the besotted look on his wife's face.

'Here's Lindsey now.' Sally finally noticed her standing in the back doorway. 'Someone here to see you, Lindsey.'

'Hello, Cole.' Lindsey was proud of her cool, unruffled greeting.

Lazily Cole straightened up from the counter and sauntered over to her. 'Hi.' Narrowing his eyes, he bent over and scrutinised her face.

'What's . . . what's the matter?' she asked breathlessly, her nerves vibrating at his nearness.

'What have you been doing?'

'Sorting stock. Why?' Pinwheels spun somewhere in her stomach region.

Cole stretched out a lone finger and lightly rubbed along her cheek bone. 'A smudge,' he said briefly.

Lindsey caught her breath at Cole's touch. Sheer willpower kept her from turning her head and capturing his finger between her lips. 'What are you doing here?' she finally managed to ask.

Cole lifted a quizzical brow. 'Don't tell me that you've already forgotten? You promised to help me with my house. The movers came today, and I thought you might like to come out and look over my stuff. Your mother said you closed at six, so here I am.'

'It's been kind of a long day,' she evaded.

'Trying to renege?' he asked coldly.

'No, no, of course not,' she denied hastily.

The expression on his face told her very clearly that he didn't believe her. Resentment rose in her throat, but before she could say anything, Cole's countenance lightened and he gave her a rueful grin. 'I'll even feed you dinner.'

'Go ahead, Lindsey,' urged Sally. 'I can close up. We aren't likely to get any more customers tonight.'

'If you're sure you don't mind.' Lindsey knew when she'd been outmanoeuvred; she might as well get it over with.

Cole's house was a surprise. She wasn't sure what she had been expecting, but not this modern cedar-clad structure situated on a grassy knoll north-east of the city. Taking full advantage of its southern exposure, a wall of windows looked out on the Air Force Academy with the Rampart Range and Pike's Peak majestic in the distance. A great room with a cathedral ceiling had furniture stacked in one corner. In the kitchen, dish packs were partially unpacked and empty cupboards stood open. An enormous bedroom and bath shared the first floor, while steps led up to a second bedroom and bath plus an open loft.

Cole said little as he showed her through the house. 'Think you can do anything with it?' he asked as he led her back to the great room.

'I'm just bursting with ideas!' she exclaimed impetuously. 'What an exciting house, Cole. How did you ever find it?'

'Pure luck. A fellow in the department got an unexpected assignment to Korea, and he was in a hurry to sell so he was willing to let it go at a loss. As you can see, it could stand some painting. The walls are in pretty sorry condition.'

'Let me see your furniture before I get too carried away. Mmm, nice.' Lindsey caressed the smooth cream leather of an enormous sofa. 'Dark walls, I think to set this off. This is German, isn't it?' she cried in delight as she spied a huge beige wardrobe painted with colourful birds and flowers.

'Yes.' Cole was kneeling on the floor, cutting ropes from a rolled up carpet. 'I'd like to use this rug in the living area here if you think it will go.' As the last rope parted, he unrolled a deep tan rug that was covered with medallion designs in various shades of blues and oranges.

'It's beautiful,' Lindsey breathed. 'We can decorate the whole house around it. Look at all the choices we'll have for colours. Show me what else you have,' she demanded, in her enthusiasm forgetting her discomfort at being with Cole.

Several hours later she looked up from where she sat on the floor, half-emptied boxes all around her. Cole lay on the sofa, a can of beer resting on his stomach, answering her eager questions. 'What lovely things you have! I'm crazy about this Japanese kimono. Were you stationed in Japan?'

'No, just TDY. I bought that for my grandmother who was bedridden at the time. She never wore it but left it hanging out where she could see it because she loved the colours.'

Lindsey traced the silk embroidery with her forefinger. 'The workmanship is exquisite. It's quite old, isn't it?'

'So the man I bought it from told me. After Grandmother died somehow it worked its way back to me. Don't know what I'll do with it.'

'I have the most splendid idea for it,' Lindsey promised.

'Whatever,' said Cole sleepily, his eyelids fluttering closed.

'Cole, have you been listening to anything I've said?' asked Lindsey suspiciously.

'Sure. Do whatever you want.' He opened one eye and squinted at her. 'Only, the sooner the better.'

'Why, of course,' she agreed with false cordiality. 'I wouldn't think of holding up your quest for the perfect wife.'

'Good.' He was unaffected by her sardonic remark.

Irked by his refusal to rise to her bait, Lindsey couldn't help but pursue the subject. 'I suppose you have the qualifications of this future help-mate of yours all figured out.'

'Certainly.'

'Beautiful, talented, charming, good with children. Have I left anything out?' she goaded, annoyed by his calm demeanour.

'You forgot a sense of humour.'

'I suppose you also require a superb hostess, superior homemaker and gourmet cook to do all the entertaining you'll want to do, to grease your way up that career ladder.'

'You're mixing your metaphors. Pretty hard to climb a greased ladder,' Cole drawled.

'Very funny,' snapped Lindsey. 'I notice you don't deny any of it.'

Cole raised up on one elbow and surveyed her through narrowed eyes. 'Not that it's any of your business,' he said smoothly, 'but as a matter of fact, I don't require cooking skills.'

'Good luck finding this paragon,' sneered Lindsey, suddenly sorry that she had ever started this conversation.

'You haven't finished listing my requirements,' said Cole coolly.

'I'm really not all that interested.' Something in his tone made her uneasy.

'Not being an applicant for the position, you mean? Just as well,' he shrugged, 'because I also want a woman with grit.'

Lindsey turned blindly away. 'Why don't you just leave me alone?' she asked tightly, her hands clenched at her side.

'Why should I do that? You can walk out any time, Lindsey. You're good at that—walking out, I mean.'

Jumping to her feet, Lindsey fled to the kitchen, out of Cole's sight. As she stood hunched over the sink, pain flowed over her in giant waves. Why not walk out? So what if Cole thought she was a quitter. She didn't have to stay around and be slashed by his razor-sharp comments. Let him find someone else to torment to relieve his frustrations!

Cole blamed the whole break-up on her, conveniently forgetting his own contributions. He had known all along about her fears, but he expected her to change for his sake, for the sake of their love. What about him? What sacrifice had he been willing to make? None. He had discounted her fears and called her a coward, a quitter.

Anger came slowly to her rescue, overriding the pain. She straightened up. Cole wanted her to quit. He wanted to be able to point an accusing finger at her, to call her a coward again. Well, she'd show him! She hadn't wanted to decorate his house, but now it would take an entire army to stop her. She'd give him a house that any normal woman would beg to call her own. That would show Cole Farrell that not only was she not a quitter, but that she would be ecstatic to see him married—if he could find some poor sucker who was too dumb to realise that all Cole wanted was another square checked off in his climb to the top. Besides, once Cole got married then she could forget him once and for all. A roll of paper towel lay near by and she grabbed up a sheet, dipped it under the cold water tap and sponged off her flushed face.

Cole's footsteps sounded in the doorway. 'Ready to leave?' he asked harshly.

Taking a deep breath, Lindsey turned. 'I'm not working at the gallery tomorrow, so we can start then, if you like. We'll need some paint, and maybe some wallpaper. I have a few ideas, but I need to know how much you're willing to spend.' She hoped Cole appreciated the businesslike tone she had tried to inject in her voice.

He gave her a startled look, but only nodded in agreement before following her on a room-by-room tour and listening to her suggestions.

The trip back to the gallery was made in silence. As Cole pulled up beside her car he spoke in clipped tones. 'I won't be able to get away before three. I'll pick you up at your apartment, so give me directions on how to get there.'

Lindsey complied in a voice as cold as his before jumping from the car. Trying to forestall any effort on

Cole's part to help her out of his sports car, in her haste she slammed the door. At his wince, she suffered a stab of conscience. 'I'm—I'm sorry,' she stammered. 'My—er—hand slipped.'

A brow lifted in utter disbelief was Cole's only answer.

Fumbling with her keys, she unlocked her car, aware that Cole was waiting to see her safely on her way. She blinked furiously to hold back the sudden tears that filled her eyes. She should have quit when Cole gave her the chance.

# CHAPTER FIVE

SHE wasn't dressing to impress Cole, Lindsey assured her twin in the mirror. So what if she were wearing a sundress of jade-green, a colour that Cole had admired on her? It just so happened that jade was her favourite colour. The fact that it brought out the soft peach in her skin and complemented her blonde hair was purely coincidental. Okay, so Cole had said this particular shade of green turned her eyes into deep, mysterious pools. That was a trite remark anyway. She peered closer into the mirror. Maybe they were a darker green when she wore jade. That settled it. She'd have to change; she couldn't let Cole think that she was wearing this dress just for him. Her slim watch caught in the folds of the dress as she reached back for the zipper. Darn! Gingerly disengaging the tangle, she caught sight of the time: almost three. The mood Cole had been in last night when he'd dropped her off, she had better not change and risk making him wait for her.

Apprehension, fear, eagerness—she would have been hard put to describe the conflicting feelings that threatened to overwhelm her as she hastily applied her lipstick. Her emotions had been up and down like a yo-yo ever since she had first seen Cole yesterday. The sound of car wheels sent her flying to the window where the sight of the familiar red Porsche in the driveway sent panic through her veins. She must be crazy to be doing this.

Striving desperately to control her churning emotions, she opened the door at Cole's knock. An appreciative gleam in his eye, quickly suppressed, made her glad that she had worn this particular dress.

'This is quite a place you have here,' he said, looking about with an appraising eye. 'Yours?' He walked over to a large quilted silk wall hanging, studying it carefully at her nod.

Lindsey tried to judge the room through his eyes. Pale blue striped wallpaper, floral curtains, chintz sofa in shades of blue and peach, pastel plaid armchairs, antique lace, a few good golden oak pieces, on the floor a light-coloured rug she'd woven, lots of plants, and her special pillows everywhere.

'It looks like you,' said Cole abruptly. He picked up a couple of pillows and scrutinised them. 'Also yours, I presume.' Not waiting for her answer, he said, 'Let's go, if you're ready.'

He stood aside, allowing her to precede him down the stairs of the old Victorian home which housed her third-floor apartment. Normally she would have admired the gay flowers that decorated the traffic islands along Nevada Avenue, but today her thoughts were too chaotic to settle on the beauty of nature. She spared only a glance for a fat robin digging for a worm beneath a pulsating sprinkler. Beside her Cole was withdrawn, speaking only to ask directions.

As they pulled up to the first store on Lindsey's list, Cole's hand on her arm prevented her from getting out of the car. 'I want to apologise. You're doing me a great favour, and I've been behaving badly.' Taking her small hand in his large one, he softly traced the lines on her palm. 'We were friends once. If I promise to behave myself, do you think we could be friends again?'

His humble tone caught her by surprise, and she eyed him suspiciously. Was this another trick? He seemed sincere. She would give him the benefit of the doubt. Helping Cole with his house would be extremely uncomfortable if he were going to continually lash out at her with hateful remarks about their past. Life would be far more pleasant if she and Cole could work together as friends. 'All right, I'm willing to try,' she agreed.

The warm smile that lit up his face at her answer evoked an answering smile from Lindsey. Maybe this wouldn't be so bad after all.

Once she was in the store, Lindsey's enthusiasm for the task at hand took all precedence over any inner misgivings she had about the project. Cole said little, readily agreeing with her purchases. The only time he showed any concern was when she turned to the wallpaper books. 'Isn't wallpaper kind of feminine?' he asked doubtfully. 'I mean, I like your apartment and all, but it's not exactly me.'

'Oh ye of little faith! Do you really think I'd put a man like you in a flowery bower like mine? I was thinking along the lines of little toy airplanes and cars,' she added mischievously.

'I'll wring your neck first,' Cole promised.

Lindsey flipped the pages. 'How about this for your bedroom?' She pointed to a deep beige wallcovering with a navy pinstripe.

He shrugged. 'My life is in your hands.'

'You are brave,' she laughed up into his face.

By the end of the afternoon, their major purchases were complete, and Lindsey sank gratefully into the car's deep bucket seat with a sigh of relief. 'Well, that's that. Now when do you want to paint? I'm not working Saturday or Sunday if that's a good time for you.'

Cole started the engine. 'Okay, I'll pick you up Saturday morning.'

'No don't bother—I'll drive out. It'll save time.'

'Whatever.' He glanced over at her. 'You're tired. Let me buy you dinner.'

'You're on. See how agreeable I am? Spending someone else's money always puts me in a good mood.'

'Then you ought to be in a really great mood,' Cole said with feeling, referring to the the big hole that she'd made in his cheque book over the past several hours.

'Did I spend too much?' asked Lindsey anxiously. 'I tried to keep within your budget.'

'I think I still have enough left to treat you to dinner,' he responded. 'Where do you want to go?'

Lindsey looked up at the blue sky filled with clouds of whipped cream. They had stopped, waiting for the green light. Beside them butterflies flitted about a patch of red blossoms, while overhead swallows swooped and darted before returning to their nests in the light-poles. It was a perfect night for a picnic.

Cole pulled the hamburgers from the bag. 'When I invited you out for dinner, this isn't exactly what I had in mind, but I have to admit it's beautiful here. What did you say this place is called?'

Lindsey looked around at the towering, pink-coloured sandstone formations below the parking lot where she and Cole sat in his car with the top off. 'Garden of the Gods. The Ute Indians used to winter here before they were sent off to Utah to the reservations. Now it's a city park as well as a Registered National Landmark. Those houses over there are part of Manitou Springs.' She pointed off in the distance. 'It used to be famous for its mineral springs, and is still a favoured tourist area. Behind it is Mount Manitou—look, you can see the train going up to the top.' She sipped her soft drink. 'The whole area was named by the Indians Manitou, or Great

Spirit, because they believed a god lived in the waters.'

'That's Pike's Peak, isn't it?'

Lindsey nodded.

'Ol' Zebulon Pike would sure be surprised if he looked down from up there today and saw all the people around.'

'He'd be even more surprised if he were up there to look down,' she retorted. 'He never made it to the top, and in fact predicted that no man ever would.'

'I'll bet you can get quite a view from up on top,' Cole mused. 'I'd like to see it.'

'You have your choice. You can climb, hike or take the train. As for view, you can see for miles, on a clear day, that is. Katherine Lee Bates was so impressed she wrote *America the Beautiful* after visiting the top.'

'Maybe, when we finish the house, you could show me some of the local sights,' he suggested.

'Maybe.' Lindsey was noncommittal. She wasn't sure that spending so much time with Cole was a wise move on her part: she was still too susceptible to his charm.

A thin slice of moon was climbing high into the darkened sky when he finally returned her to her apartment. 'I enjoyed the sightseeing. Tomorrow's Friday. Why don't I pick you up after work, and you can introduce me to more of your fair city.'

'I'm sorry, but I already have other plans,' Lindsey said.

A brow lifted in utter disbelief.

'Really I do,' she rushed to explain. 'Ross asked me to go to an old movie down at the Showboat.'

'Ross? Oh yes, your red-haired flame,' Cole drawled. 'Still hanging in there, is he? Has he gathered up enough courage yet?'

'I don't know what you mean.'

'Sure you do,' he said easily. 'Has he decided yet that

the time is right to ask you to marry him?'

'Not that it's any of your business,' said Lindsey stiffly, 'but we haven't discussed it since my return.'

'In other words, he's afraid that you'll say no,' said Cole knowingly.

'Ross is a sensible, level-headed individual . . .'

'With both feet on the ground,' he interjected irrepressibly.

'Yes, if you insist, with both feet on the ground,' she coldly agreed with him, adding, 'He doesn't like to rush into things.'

'He must be very sure of you,' Cole commented.

'With cause,' she retorted, jumping from the car. Without a word Cole slammed his car into gear and sped from the driveway in a spate of loose gravel.

Triumph wrestled with uneasy conscience as Lindsey unlocked the door at the top of the staircase. The startled look on Cole's face almost quieted the qualms she felt about lying to him. The truth was, whether Ross was sure of her or not, she had given him no cause to be so.

Returning from Germany, Lindsey had been too depressed and unhappy to be interested in any kind of social life. But as her mother had become concerned about her withdrawal from her normal activities, she had made an effort to get out more, and gradually she and Ross had drifted back into their old dating pattern. Although Ross had never pressed her for an explanation, he seemed to sense that Lindsey had somehow changed, and appeared to be content to ignore the subject of their future. In the meantime, he was an agreeable date, and at least going about with him kept her mother's questions at bay.

Maybe not so agreeable, she thought in irritation the next evening as she and Ross sat in the theatre waiting for the movie to begin. Excited by the challenge of decorating Cole's house, she had been eager to answer Ross's enquiry as to how she'd spent the previous day. Little did she realise that he would instantly take exception to her activities. Not blatantly, no; he knew better than to state outright that he didn't like her decorating the house of a man he knew nothing about. Instead he contented himself with wondering how Caroline and Charles felt about her spending so much time with some strange man, or bemoaning the possibility that her work for Cole would interfere with the time she could spend with him.

By the time the theatre darkened and the movie began, Lindsey was heartily sick of his insinuations. Cole would never have hinted around and expected her to understand and heed his wishes. He had always been open and truthful with Lindsey.

Which was more than she was being with Ross. The uncomfortable conviction began to grow on her that she was using Ross much as she had used Cole. She had never considered herself a selfish person, but there was no denying that she was trading on Ross's affection for her to take her mind off Cole as much as to calm her mother's fears. Lindsey was disgusted by her own behaviour. The time had come to gently ease Ross out of her life. It wasn't fair for him to waste his time and energy on a woman who had fallen in love with another man. The fact that her love affair with Cole had a disastrous ending was no excuse for allowing Ross to think that their relationship might develop into any kind of serious commitment.

Convincing Ross that there was no future for the two of them proved to be impossible. She should have realised that his red hair and Scots ancestry were indicators of a bulldog stubbornness. She just needed to get Cole out of her system he argued—an argument that stunned her with its shrewd perception, since she didn't once mention Cole's name, and had had no idea that Ross had been aware that he even had a rival. She had finally succeeded in getting him to go home, although his attitude as he left strongly suggested that he still had a great deal he wished to say on the subject of their parting. Lindsey didn't believe for a minute that Ross was resigned to his dismissal, and she was guiltily aware that she had much to answer for in her treatment of him.

A sleepless night left Lindsey groggy and bad-tempered the next morning. Several cups of coffee were necessary before she felt able to face the day ahead of her. Dressed in stained and tattered painting clothes, she made the drive to Cole's house in record time. As she pulled up to the wooden structure, it occurred to her that she should have called first. Maybe he wouldn't even be up.

Putting off approaching his door, Lindsey leaned against the side of her car and looked about her. This late in June only a few violet blue pentstemons remained, but lavender and white daisies were unfurling their delicate blooms to colour the landscape. Clusters of stonecrop were yellow splashes in areas dried brown by the hot summer sun. Beneath some scrub oak a rufous-sided towhee made rustling sounds as he scratched in the weeds. A chickadee darting overhead called out his name and nearby a pair of small grey nuthatches tapped a pine tree. The morning dew had already dissipated, but the damp smell of pine drifted past Lindsey on a slight breeze.

'Hey there, lazybones, did you come out here to work or just stand around and daydream?' Cole's laughing comment jerked her upright.

'Don't I look like I'm dressed for work?' She pirouetted for his approval.

'You don't look like any painter I've ever seen. Do you paint in that outfit, or use it to clean your brushes?'

'I'll have you know that this outfit is a veteran of every paint job I've ever done. Here's Mom's dining room, and here's my bedroom trim, and here's . . .'

'Whoa! I believe you.' By now Lindsey had reached the front step and Cole grabbed her arm and rushed her inside. 'While other people were goofing off last night,' he cast a significant look her way, 'I was busy. Come and see what you think.' Leading her to the master bedroom and bath, he stood aside to allow her to enter first.

Lindsey stood transfixed as the extent of Cole's labours dawned on her. 'You must have worked half the night!' she gasped. 'The wallpaper looks wonderful,' she began, abruptly halting as she took in the enormous bed that dominated the bedroom. Made entirely of brass and chrome, it had thin square posts at each corner rising almost to the ceiling, where they were connected by a thin rectangular frame. Stark and modern, the four-poster bed only hinted at being influenced by the past.

'What's wrong?' Cole asked. 'Don't you like my waterbed?'

'A waterbed!' Lindsey echoed in surprise, before giving him a sly look, 'The bachelor's trademark.' At his noncommittal shrug, she added, 'The bed is stunning, and it looks terrific with this wallpaper. And that enormous old armoire provides a wonderful contrast to both. Your grandmother's? I didn't notice it or the bed the other day.'

'Yes, it was hers. I forgot to show them to you. The wardrobe was hidden behind some cartons, and the bed was still in pieces.' He looked around. 'But I know you well enough to know that there's something here you don't like.'

'Well,' Lindsey hesitated before blurting out, 'I hate the sheets and bedspread.'

Cole shrugged. 'That's easy enough to remedy. Buy new ones.'

Belatedly she remembered tact. 'It's not that I hate them, but they really don't go with the bed and the wallpaper.'

'You don't like rainbows? I have a feeling that you're going hate my towels, too,' he said in resignation as she headed towards the bathroom.

He was right. Lindsey saw at once that the towels, imprinted with Victorian nudes in black on a white background, were entirely unsuitable for the room which Cole had once again wallpapered beautifully, this time in a navy and beige tiny geometric print.

'And before you say anything, the towels were a gift from my mother,' he informed her virtuously.

Since she had been on the verge of uttering a sarcastic comment, his remark effectively took the wind from her sails and she contented herself with saying that she would look for towels when she shopped for new sheets. 'Maybe we can use the towels in the upstairs bathroom. We bought a pale salmon paint for it.'

'Speaking of paint . . .' said Cole suggestively.

'Slavedriver! I'm coming,' and with one last appreciative look at the bed, she followed him to the kitchen where he was stirring the paint.

'You know what would look really terrific on that bed?'

'What,' asked Lindsay absently, her mind on the job ahead as she sorted brushes and prepared the paint roller.

'The quilt hanging in your apartment. Why don't you sell it to me?'

Lindsey thought about the hours and effort she had put into the large hanging, her favourite work. Composed of tiny squares of silk in shades of blues, greens, browns and variations of orange from the brightest tangerine to the palest peach, the quilt was an abstract landscape of a Colorado sunset. Besides having won first place in a juried craft show, the quilt had been a labour of love. 'It's not for sale,' she said at last.

'Not for sale to me, or not for sale at all?' asked Cole after a moment.

'Not to anyone,' Lindsey declared. 'Honestly, I love that hanging, and I just couldn't bear to part with it.'

Carefully Cole poured paint into the shallow roller pan. 'Why don't I commission you to make me a quilt for my bed?' he asked thoughtfully.

'That's awfully expensive,' she warned.

'You'll never get rich trying to talk customers out of buying a Lindsey Keegan original,' Cole chided her. 'You make the quilt, and I'll worry about making enough money to pay for it.'

'If you're certain . . .' At his decisive nod, she added, 'Give me some time to think about it and develop a few ideas and sketches.'

Satisfied to have won his point, Cole concentrated on the task at hand and soon he and Lindsey were hard at work transforming dingy white walls.

'Oh, pain!' Lindsey moaned, getting slowly up from the floor where she'd been painting skirtingboards for the past hour. Hand rubbing the small of her back, she worked her neck around, trying to get rid of kinks. 'I'd never make it as a house painter!'

Cole looked down from the ladder, a sarcastic lift to his

brows. 'Aren't you the one who said, and I quote, "Painting is so simple, we can cover those walls in no time"?'

Lindsey winced. 'I have my stupid days,' she confessed. She strolled over to the foot of the ladder and examined the wall where Cole had finished. 'The man lied. I think we're going to have to put on a second coat of this navy.'

'Don't tell me that while I'm on top of a ladder,' Cole pleaded. 'I might be tempted to leap to my death.'

'You'd be lucky to twist an ankle, considering you're only three steps up,' she retorted.

'All heart, that's what I love about you,' he said, stepping down from the ladder.

Lindsey looked at him sharply at his use of the word love. The bland look on his face convinced her that he'd meant nothing by it, but was merely using a common expression.

'C'mon.' His voice jerked her from unpleasant thoughts. 'I'm starving. How about a little lunch?'

'Who's going to fix it?' asked Lindsey suspiciously.

Cole laughed. 'Don't worry. I picked up some bread, cheese and cold cuts yesterday.' As he washed his hands, he added with a straight face, 'There's too much work to do here to risk letting you cook.'

The paint-covered rag that she fired made a direct hit on Cole's back. 'Very funny!'

He just smiled and made her a tall glass of iced tea. Lindsey found some clean rags and covered a couple of chairs with them for protection. Soon she and Cole were munching away, Lindsey discovering that she was ravenous.

'It's looking good,' Cole observed, studying the living room area. 'I'm going to like it.'

'I promise you will,' said Lindsey earnestly. 'I know it's hard to visualise now with newspaper all over the floor and the furniture covered with plastic, but it's going to look modern and comfortable with just a touch of masculinity, though not so much that a woman would be overpowered by it. That way, when you get married, it won't take much for your wife to change it to be suitable for her, too.'

'And if she doesn't know what to do, we'll just call on you again,' Cole said with a disarming grin.

Piqued by his remark, Lindsey pushed aside the rest of her lunch, her appetite gone. 'I'll get back to painting,' she said tersely.

The remainder of the afternoon passed smoothly enough. She convinced herself that he had not meant to be provocative with his remarks, and that she was too sensitive to his every comment. Cole seemed content to stick with non-controversial topics, and conversation was easy and wide-ranging. He spoke of growing up, the only boy with three older sisters, and Lindsey told stories out of her past. Neither made any allusions to his future or their mutual past. Time passed swiftly, and Lindsey was startled when Cole's grandfather clock pealed loudly seven times.

'I had no idea it was that late,' she said, stretching aching muscles. 'However,' she triumphantly slapped on one last brush worth of paint, 'I'm through in here for today.'

'Slowcoach,' called Cole from the kitchen. 'I finished hours ago.'

'You did not!'

'Would you believe five minutes ago?'

Grimacing as sore muscles protested her every movement, Lindsey collapsed on to the plastic-covered sofa. 'I can't decide whether to die now or wait until I wash out my brush.'

'Here, give it to me.'

Not bothering to protest, Lindsey handed it over, and rubbed the back of her neck.

'Stiff?' Cole enquired.

'Uh-huh.'

'Let me rub it.' Coming closer, he took one look at her and shouted with laughter.

'What's so funny?' she asked indignantly, wiping her face with her paint-smeared hand.

'No, no,' Cole gasped, 'you're making it worse! You look like you were getting ready to do an Indian war dance, only you tripped and fell in the paint. Not to mention that all your freckles have turned navy blue.'

'Go ahead and laugh. I'm too tired to stop you.'

Cole sobered up immediately. 'Poor Lindsey, you look exhausted. Here, let me.' Grabbing a wet towel, he briskly rubbed her nose and cheeks. 'Shut your eyes,' he ordered. 'Luckily we were using a water-based paint, otherwise you'd have to shower in turpentine.'

Leaning back against the sofa, Lindsey weakly submitted to Cole's ministrations. The stress of spending the day working so closely with him, combined with the sheer physical fatigue from painting, left her feeling totally drained.

Sinking deep into the sofa, she was vaguely aware that the tempo of Cole's rubbing had slowed almost to a gentle caress. The day hadn't been all that bad. For the most part he had refrained from sarcasm and remembered his agreement for a truce the duration of the redecorating. Tomorrow. All she had to do was get through tomorrow, and then she could forget Cole once and for all. Her head slid lower.

'Lindsey, wake up!'

Lindsey struggled to raise leaden eyelids. It wasn't enough that every muscle in her body shrieked with pain, but someone was shaking her every bone. She wished whoever it was would stop.

'Come on, Sleeping Beauty, wake up. Dinner's ready.'

The voice didn't belong to her mother. Were her eyes glued shut? She willed them open. Cole stood leaning over her, one hand on the back of the sofa, the other gripping her shoulder. 'Go away,' she ordered drowsily.

'As soon as you open your eyes, I will.'

'They're open,' she insisted.

'All the way,' he said remorselessly.

She squeezed her eyelids tightly shut. Cole needn't think he could boss her around.

'Lindsey.' His voice was so stern. Did he think he was directing his troops? 'You've got thirty seconds to open those eyes and go and get ready for dinner, or I'm going to carry you over to the table.'

That didn't sound like an idle threat. Her eyes popped open.

'I thought that would get your attention,' said Cole in satisfaction. 'You have five minutes to wash before I put dinner on the table.'

'I'm not eating dinner here.' She scowled at him as he turned back to the kitchen.

He didn't even bother to turn around as he answered her absently. 'If you'd rather eat with paint all over your hands, that, of course, is up to you.'

'I'm not eating here,' she insisted stubbornly.

'Four minutes,' he said, his back to her as he stirred something on the stove.

Lindsay stuck her tongue out at him before heading for the bathroom. He needn't think he had intimidated her! It was simply that dinner smelled so good, and she suddenly remembered that all she had in her refrigerator was some yogurt and a couple of over-ripe apples. Besides, she was too tired to argue right now.

Cole was too experienced a tactician to allow any triumph to cross his face as she dutifully sat down at the table. Delicious smells wafted from the plate he set in front of her, and Lindsey swiftly forgave him his dictatorial manner, at least, for the moment.

'Beef Stroganoff! This is delicious,' she enthused as she took a bite. 'Imagine having a husband who can cook like this. I envy your wife.'

Cole's brows shot clear to his hairline in disbelief.

Far too belatedly, Lindsey's brain caught up with her words.

Aghast, she choked on a noodle. 'I mean . . . you know . . . a man who can cook . . . any woman . . .' Her tongue tripped over itself as she tried to explain away her embarrassing remark.

Cole leaned back on his chair, coolly surveying her over the rim of his wine glass, a mocking look in his eyes.

She attacked her dinner furiously, and silence reigned at the table. Hidden by that silence, her thoughts flowed fast and furious. It was a compliment, she fumed. He should have been flattered instead of giving her that nasty, arrogant look. She thrust her plate aside. 'Thank you for dinner. I'll do the dishes.'

'The hell you will,' he answered in a deceptively mild voice.

'And what does that mean?' she asked icily.

'Just what you think it means,' he returned tersely. 'I paid a pretty penny for these dishes in Quimper, France, and I have no intention of letting you slam them around to exorcise your own little private demons.'

'You are the most hateful, arrogant . . .'

Cole pushed back his chair and came around the table. 'And you are acting like a child who's missed her nap. You're tired. Time you were in bed.' He pulled back her chair. 'I put clean sheets on the waterbed for you.'

Lindsey's mouth dropped open to her chin. 'You did what?' she gasped.

'You heard me.'

'If you think I have any intention of sleeping with you . . .'

'I don't.'

'But—but you . . . you . . . just said . . .' she stammered.

'I said I put clean sheets on the waterbed. I did not say that I intend to share it, a conclusion to which your mind jumped with such flattering speed that I can't help but wonder if you've been considering it.'

'Why, you——' As quick as her hand was, his was quicker. An iron grip locked her arm behind her back, forcing her body up next to his. Torn between fear and anticipation, Lindsey forced herself to look Cole straight in the face. 'Let me go,' she said coldly.

'Why? So you can slap me?' he taunted. 'I have a better idea.' He lowered his head.

'No,' she cried breathlessly. Pressed against his solid chest, she could feel the pulsating of his heart, and she wondered if he could feel the way hers raced at his touch. She was drowning in his fathomless blue eyes, hypnotised by the approach of his relentless lips. He uttered a soft, exultant laugh before capturing the mouth that quivered so near to his. Weariness was immediately replaced by a quickening of the blood. Lindsey's senses all seemed to rejuvenate at once, tinglingly alive. Cole toyed with her lips, nibbling the corners and gently biting the flesh. Lindsey could taste the wine he'd drunk with dinner. Her body softened and shaped itself to fit his firm, masculine contours. He must have freed her hand because it joined her other one in trailing through his hair, the brown strands like silk between her fingers.

Tiring of the gentle assault on her lips, Cole set out to conquer new battlefields, and a thrusting tongue demanded and won entry to the soft moistness of her mouth. He unbuttoned her shirt and bra allowing cool air to brush sensuously across the pink tips of tingling breasts before he warmed the hard nubs with his possessive hands. The contact ignited a flame which raced to the centre of Lindsey's being, where it burned, hot and wanting. Her own hands found their way to his shirt front, and she slipped her arms inside. His back felt cool to her feverish touch, and she sensuously traced his muscles with her fingertips, delighting in his answering quiver.

Cole's hands, having won control of her breasts, now abandoned them, and she moaned in displeasure. Pushing her away, he roughly buttoned up her shirt, and her eyelids flew up in bewilderment.

'There are clean towels in the bathroom if you want to take a shower before you go to bed,' he said hoarsely. 'I'll sleep upstairs on the couch.'

Feverish from Cole's lovemaking, and shaking with desire, Lindsey was incapable of speech. Shamed that her body had betrayed her, she found her eyes had filled with tears, and she couldn't stop the one that escaped.

Cole reached towards her and flicked it from her face with a gentle finger. 'You're tired. You'll feel better after a long night's sleep.'

The soft, kind words broke the dam that Lindsey had

been holding on her emotions, and tears flowed down her cheeks. She was so confused. What did he want of her? Through a film of water she saw him hand her a handkerchief. Accepting it, she blew her nose loudly.

'Better?'

She nodded, refusing to meet his eyes. He must think she was some kind of fool. She was so tired. If she were just home in bed . . .

'You're exhausted. It would be madness to let you drive home on the interstate in the condition you're in. A quick shower and you can be asleep in ten minutes.'

The thought of bed was heavenly. She sniffed. 'I can't stay.'

'Why not?' he asked in exasperation.

'I don't have a nightgown.'

'I'm sure I can come up with a suitable alternative.' He forced the words past tightly clenched lips, and Lindsey sensed the tension that lurked just below his surface calm.

All of a sudden, his suggestion seemed the only sensible answer. She was exhausted. She did have to come back tomorrow to finish painting. It was silly for her to get so worked up over sleeping in his bed; he had already assured her that he wouldn't be sharing it with her. Abruptly, she capitulated. 'All right.'

If Cole were elated by his victory, he allowed none of his feelings to show, merely leading Lindsey to the bathroom where he pointed out soap, shampoo and towels, and determined that she had all she needed, before he left her to her shower. The warm water cascading over her tired and aching muscles did much to restore her to normal spirits. Stepping out from the shower and into the adjoining bedroom, she discovered Cole's 'suitable alternative'. A man's large T-shirt was laid out on the bed. She hastily towelled dry and yanked the shirt over wet and tangled curls. A comb of Cole's lay on the sink, and she tugged it through her hair, restoring some semblance of order. Wearily she crossed the room to the light switch and turned off the light. She ought to think about Cole's kiss and her own reaction, but she was so tired. She'd think about it in the morning. The Greek flokati on the floor felt good to her bare feet as she stumbled in the dark over to the bed. As she tumbled in, her last thought before she fell sound asleep was that she would never be able to sleep in a waterbed.

From somewhere outside, a house wren was trilling his morning aria. Shafts of light evaded the closed window shade and chased golden motes over the bed. The entire world seemed to be up and about its daily business. Except for Lindsey. Moving was too painful. How could one possibly get so stiff from wielding a paint brush? Rolling carefully over on to her stomach, she wondered if Cole were suffering the same morning-after effects. She ought to get up. The enticing aroma of coffee wafted into the bedroom. Cole was already up—she'd get up, too. In just a minute.

She evidently dozed off, because the next thing she knew there were voices coming from the direction of the kitchen. Cole must have the radio or television on. Stretching gingerly on the unfamiliar bed, Lindsey let her mind drift back over the previous night. If she'd had any doubts before whether she was still in love with Cole, last night had certainly dispelled them. Remembering the feel of his hands cradling her breasts sent sparks of desire shooting clear to her toes. Restlessly she moved in the bed, causing a minor tidal wave. What had Cole thought about her wanton response? He'd certainly had no trouble sending her off to bed alone. Maybe the truth was that he wasn't all that interested. Although he'd made his share of sarcastic comments about her rejecting his marriage proposal, he hadn't once repeated it. If he really loved her, wouldn't he be trying to change her mind? Instead he was actually looking around for someone else to propose to. If that didn't prove to her how little he had cared for her . . .

'Forget the painting, Cole. It's a perfect day for a picnic. I thought we could drive up in the Rampart Range area.' The unknown voice, female, yanked Lindsey from her unprofitable thoughts. Cole wasn't listening to the radio; he had company. Sitting up in bed—not easy when one was unfamiliar with a waterbed, Lindsey craned her neck to hear Cole's reply. Would he disclose her presence? The bedroom door, open only a crack, sufficiently hid her, at the same time providing her with ample opportunity to eavesdrop. Unfortunately, the unknown visitor must be nearer the door than Cole was, because, try as she might, Lindsey was unable to hear his reply.

'I know what . . .' The woman had walked away from the door and whatever she knew was lost in the whir of a blender.

Lindsey hopped out of bed, and on bare feet, stole quietly to the door. Positioning one eye at the crack, she could barely make out Cole with his back to her, doing something on the kitchen counter. Angling her head first in one direction and then another, she was finally successful in locating Cole's visitor. A tall, dark haired woman. Lindsey knew she'd seen her somewhere. She scrunched up her forehead trying to pin down the elusive memory. Of course: she had seen her crossing the terrazzo at the Academy the day she'd seen Cole there. At the time, Lindsey had admired the woman in her trim blue uniform, saucy cap and confident air.

Now, studying her in tight blue jeans and snug-fitting tank top, she decided that the woman was too aggressive and self-assured. Lindsey disliked her on sight. Did the woman really think that Cole would be impressed by her showing up on his doorstep with the morning paper? Judging from the smug look on her face, she apparently did. The appreciative look on Cole's face as his eyes boldly roamed her over-exposed figure told Lindsey what it was about the woman that impressed him. Leave it to a man to be taken in by the cover and miss the fact that the book was a loser. The next thing she knew, he would totally forget that Lindsey was in the bedroom and that they had planned to paint today. If he thought she would change all her plans and come back another day to help him just because of some over-stimulated female warrior, he had another think coming!

Ostentatiously stretching and rubbing sleep from her eyes, Lindsey walked down the hall to the kitchen. A quick glance in the hall mirror assured her that although her face was wiped free of make-up, and her hair badly tousled from a night's sleep, she didn't look an old hag. Cole's undershirt covered her to mid-thigh, the white fabric providing a pleasing contrast with her golden tan. 'Morning, Cole,' she slurred her words sleepily. 'That coffee smells divine.' Blinking drowsily, she ambled over to where Cole stood, an astonished look on his face. Biting her lower lip to prevent untimely laughter, she rubbed her cheek against his arm. 'I don't know about you,' she pouted, 'but my body is sore all over after last night. You're a real slavedriver!' Beneath her cheek she could feel the muscles tensing in his arm.

He shifted, tucking her into his side. 'I don't believe you've met Cheryl Davis. Cheryl is in my department at the Academy.'

'Oh,' Lindsey feigned surprise at seeing the other woman, 'I didn't realise we had company, Cole. I would have—er—dressed.' A glance downward called attention to her scanty attire.

'I'm sure you would have,' said Cole drily before introducing her to his colleague.

Each woman echoed the other's insincere pleasure at the encounter. Lindsey walked over to the cupboard and selected a coffee cup, proving without a doubt that she was totally familiar with Cole's home. Smiling vaguely at the other woman over the rim of her cup, Lindsey was content to let her actions speak for her.

Cheryl received the message, and was goaded into speech. 'I came to see if Cole was interested in going on a picnic,' she explained stiffly. 'I thought he might like to take a break from his house-painting chores. I didn't realise that he already had plans.' The tone of her voice made the word 'plans' sound somehow obscene.

'How thoughtful of you,' Lindsey said with sugary sweetness. 'It's too bad that we're only half through, isn't it, Cole?'

'Perhaps another time.' Cole's face had stiffened with annoyance at Cheryl's insinuation, and ignoring Lindsey's facetious question, he led the way to the front door, Cheryl having no option except to follow him.

'Nice meeting you,' Lindsey called after them, determined to have the last word. From the kitchen window she could see Cole talking, his arm holding open the car door as Cheryl slid under the wheel. Whatever he was saying seemed to meet with the other woman's approval, as she suddenly smiled in response. Cole shut her door, and stood in the drive watching her out of sight before he turned back towards the house. Whatever charm he'd been using to placate Cheryl was gone, wiped from his face by the anger that leapt across the open yard towards Lindsey.

Belatedly Lindsey saw her rash behaviour through Cole's eyes. He had every reason to be furious with her. What business was it of hers to decide who Cole should date or marry? She had given up any right to question Cole's behaviour when she'd turned down his marriage proposal. Why had she succumbed to such an idiotic impulse this morning? If only the floor would split open and swallow her up before Cole came in. Too late, she thought hysterically, at the sound of the door closing. She'd have to brazen it out, pretending that her presence in his kitchen dressed only in his revealing undershirt was totally innocent. Taking a swallow of coffee, she addressed the air near his right ear, 'This coffee is delicious. All I know how to fix is instant.'

Not bothering to answer her, Cole propped his long length against the refrigerator and subjected her scantily clad body to long and careful perusal. With heightened colour, Lindsey stared back at him, determined not to let him disconcert her. Gathering his muscles like a tiger about to spring, Cole stood up and walked towards her. She stiffened in preparation for his attack. He reached around her and lifted the coffee pot. Slowly he filled his mug with coffee, then cream and sugar. Picking up a spoon, he stirred the contents of his mug with careful deliberation. When he finally spoke, his voice was deceptively mild. 'The last thing I expected was a dog-in-the-manger attitude from you.'

Lindsey flinched at Cole's contemptuous assessment of her actions. Not that he was wrong. Hot tears of shame filled her eyes. 'I'm sorry,' she choked.

'If you're worried about your reputation,' the slow,

measured tones pelted down like hailstones on Lindsey's already sore conscience, 'I explained to Cheryl that appearances can lie, and that you are not my lover, merely my interior decorator. She decided it was in her own best interests to believe me.'

'Meaning that she wants you herself?' Lindsey rashly retorted, wiping away an angry tear.

Match to dynamite. An iron band swept her tight up against Cole's chest. His heavy jeans rubbed against her bare legs. 'Jealous?' he taunted, not waiting for her answer as he raised her chin with a rough thumb. It was more a punishment than a kiss, and Lindsey fought to escape Cole's relentless mouth. His body held her prisoner against the cold enamel of the refrigerator, while one hand gripped the back of her head, subduing her struggles. The other hand boldly roamed beneath the T-shirt, exploring the curves of her hips.

Tension built up to an explosive pitch in Lindsey's body. The determination to fight Cole warred with her need to satisfy more basic desires. She offered only token objection when he grabbed the neckline of his T-shirt, ripping it to her navel. Already warm and heavy with desire, her breasts seemed to swell to fill his large palms. She moaned with frustration when his stroking fingers failed to calm her quivering nerves but only served to heighten the sexual excitement that raced through her body. No longer in control of her thoughts or emotions, her woman's age-old instincts took over, guiding her fingers to slip inside the back waistband of Cole's jeans, while at the same time she ground her hips against his. A responsive shudder tore through Cole's body and his hands convulsively tightened around Lindsey's breasts, surprising a sudden gasp from her. Grasping the torn edges of her flimsy attire, he severed it completely.

Stunned by the harsh ripping sound, Lindsey blinked open eyes still clouded by passion. The look of barely controlled rage on Cole's face brought her abruptly to her senses. Cole was not participating in an act of love; this was an act of revenge. 'No, Cole, please.' The pleading words were forced past trembling lips as she endeavoured to gather the tattered remnants of Cole's T-shirt about her shaking body.

His strength made a mockery of her puny efforts as he easily pulled her back against his body. 'Quitting again, Lindsey?' he taunted. 'As usual, after starting something, you want to cut and run, but this time I'm not going to let you.' His voice was cold and dispassionate, freezing her to the very marrow of her bones.

'I didn't mean to start anything, and you know it.' Her voice matched his for ice. 'And I have no intention of letting you finish it!'

'We'll see, won't we,' he said ominously as his head lowered.

She twisted, denying him access to her lips. 'What will we see, Cole? That you can only make it with an unwilling woman? When I was willing, you rejected me without turning a hair. Do you need to use force to add spice to your love life?'

A large hand jerked her face around to face his, bringing quick tears to her eyes. 'You have a vicious tongue, Lindsey. I ought to beat you for that crack.'

'Sure, why not?' she cried. 'Obviously that's how you get your kicks. You've been dying to do violence to me since I got up this morning!'

Cole laughed, a sound more chilling than the refrigerator at her back. 'That's not what I've been dying to do since you got up, and you know it.' Releasing her hands, he firmly grasped the severed edges of her inadequate garment and overlapped them, covering her nakedness. 'You have exactly five seconds to get that half-naked body into the bedroom and start getting some clothes on it, or I *will* be tempted to violence. For the first time in my life, I might add.' The last words were uttered through gritted teeth.

She didn't need five seconds.

# CHAPTER SIX

A MUCH chastened Lindsey emerged from the bedroom some time later. She had considered hiding in there all day, but she knew that Cole would drag her out if he had to. She would make her apologies and then go home. There was no denying that Cole's anger was justified. How could she have done anything so stupid? Facing him would be one of the most difficult things she'd ever done.

He barely glanced up when she walked in. 'Your breakfast is ready.'

'Cole, I . . .' she began.

'Eat first. Then we'll talk.'

The breakfast that Cole had prepared was delicious, and Lindsey was surprised to find that she was able to eat every bit of it, So much for an uneasy conscience making you lose your appetite! Resolutely she tossed aside her crumpled napkin and faced Cole. He was eyeing her over the rim of his coffee mug, an enigmatic expression on his face. Lindsey took a deep breath. 'I'm sorry, Cole. That was really childish of me.'

'Why did you do it, Lindsey?'

'I don't know,' she cried. 'Yes, I do know.' Honesty forced her to face up to the truth. 'That's what's so awful about it. I was jealous, and I have no right to be.' She fiddled with the silverware beside her plate. 'I wanted that . . . that woman . . . to think that . . . that . . .'

'That we were lovers,' Cole interjected coolly.

'Yes. And—and I don't have the right to . . . to drive

136

away other women. When I woke up, and heard her talking—well, something just came over me. I don't blame you for being so angry with me.' She glanced up from beneath lowered lids. Cole regarded her steadily, saying nothing. 'I'll leave now. You . . . you can probably still make it for her picnic . . .'

'You could have the right if you wanted it.' Casually spoken, the words demonstrated more than any actions could the hidden dangers in the path that she and Cole had chosen. How could two people who had been so in love deny that love and profess to be mere friends?

'It won't work, Cole. I just can't.'

'Can't what?'

'Marry you. That is what you meant, isn't it?' At his nod, she continued, 'We should have just let things be the way the they were when I left Germany. I haven't changed my mind. I can't marry you. I just couldn't bear the worry, the uncertainty.' She sighed. 'You obviously haven't changed your mind about the flying. I won't take you on your terms, and yet this morning shows that I'm not willing to let someone else take you. Our friendship now is a mistake, and this morning proves it. I think I ought to leave now and . . .'

Suddenly and unexpectedly, Cole laughed. 'Oh, no you don't! You promised to help me finish painting today, and I intend to hold you to that promise.'

'Then you're not still mad?'

'We'll take up what I am at a later date.' With a swift yank on her chair, he pulled her out from the table. 'Come on, lazybones, let's get to work. All this gabbing, and the day is wasting away.'

Hours later, Lindsey plopped down on the floor. 'I'm exhausted, but it looks terrific, don't you think?'

Cole looked up from cleaning the paintbrushes at the

sink. 'Thanks to you, it does. You've been working like a real trouper, and don't think I don't appreciate it.' Concentrating on his task, he lightly added, 'Dare I guess, expiation for your sins?'

'I guess you could say that it was my way of apologising to you,' she admitted. 'I don't normally make such a fool of myself.'

'Thank heaven for small favours!'

'How long do I have to go on apologising for what I did?' Lindsey asked crossly. 'You didn't behave so well yourself.'

Cole threw up his hands in surrender. 'Point taken. We'll consider the subject closed. Why don't you go and clean up while I finish here? That smear of paint on your nose keeps tempting me to come over and kiss it.'

Furiously Lindsey rubbed at her nose, transferring a streak of yellow to her palm. 'Did I get it?' She would ignore the comment about kissing.

'Actually, you made it worse. I think you have time for a quick shower before company arrives.'

'Company?'

The sound of a car motor prevented his answer. He craned his head to look out of the window. 'Too late. Here they come now.'

'Oh no!' Lindsey dashed for the bathroom.

Cole's next words stopped her cold. 'When you come out, wear more than a T-shirt, okay?'

'I thought that subject was closed.'

He winced. 'Sorry, that was a low blow. I promise I won't mention it again.' A loud knock on the door propelled Lindsey on her way. Cole's last words floated down the hall behind her. 'I don't promise not to remember it, however. You've got great legs.'

Lindsey backed up against the bathroom door, her

muscles trembling. A charming Cole could be even more devastating to her system than an angry one. He had her so confused. Why couldn't he have a safe and sane job like being a stockbroker, or teacher, or even a lawyer like Ross? Then he wouldn't be Cole, an inner voice answered.

She was in the shower scrubbing furiously away at the paint that spotted her body in the most unexpected places when the realisation dawned on her that she didn't have any other clothes to put on. Expecting to go home last night, she only had what she'd worn to paint in. Well, whoever Cole's guests were, they would just have to accept her in all her paint-covered glory.

Stepping from the shower, she wrapped herself in one of Cole's enormous towels, smiling at the prim and proper nudes printed on it. A gift from his mother, indeed! Navy towels would look sharp against the wallpaper, she decided, with maybe some turquoise accents. Mulling ideas over in her head, she didn't immediately grasp that someone was already in Cole's bedroom, bouncing on the waterbed. 'Mother!' Lindsey stopped in astonishment.

'Isn't this bed fun?' Caroline asked gleefully. 'I wonder how Charles would feel about our buying a waterbed.'

Lindsey dropped weakly into a wicker chair in the corner. 'What are you doing here?'

'Didn't Cole tell you? He called last night and told me you were too tired to drive into town.'

'Cole called you and told you that I was spending the night here last night?'

'Yes. Wasn't that sweet of him?'

'No! I'm twenty-three years old. I don't need my mother's permission to spend the night at a friend's house.'

'Of course you don't, darling. I expect that Cole just didn't want us to worry. If I called late and you weren't home, I mean. Not that I check up on you or anything,' added Caroline hastily, correctly interpreting the storm clouds on Lindsey's face. 'Then Cole called back today and suggested that Charles and I drive out this evening to see the results of your massive redecorating job. I brought you some clothes to change into,' she placated, pointing to some of Lindsey's things spread beside her on the bed.

Pleased to have clean underwear and a paint-free dress, not to mention cosmetics, Lindsey grudgingly decided that she could ignore her mother's interference this time. 'I take it Cole didn't have much trouble persuading you to come,' she said drily as she slipped into the silken garments her mother handed her.

'I even volunteered to bring dinner, I was so anxious to see what you were doing. And I must say, I'm impressed. I have to check on dinner, but when you finish getting dressed you can give me the grand tour.'

Her mother's departure left Lindsey with plenty to think about. So Cole had called her parents today. Obviously he was making sure that there was no repetition of what had happened last night or this morning. Was he worried that she would throw herself into his arms again? He should be so lucky, she defiantly told her image in the bathroom mirror.

Cole didn't have a hair drier, and her mother had omitted to bring Lindsey's, so her hair was drying in tight curls over all her head, giving her the appearance of an over-age moppet. At least the dress Caroline had selected dispelled any childish image with its missing back and plunging front. Lindsey frowned. Maybe the front plunged a little too much. Now was not exactly the time to be wearing a sexy dress. Biting her lip in exasperation, she could imagine Cole's thoughts on seeing her in it. Well, there was no help for it. A thorough search of Cole's closet and bed failed to disclose the dress's matching jacket. Apparently Caroline had seen no need to bring it on this warm summer evening.

Reluctantly Lindsey returned to the living room. Pausing at the threshold, she answered Cole's slow appraisal of her appearance with a defiant glare.

'I like your dress,' he said in dulcet tones.

Lindsey was not deceived. 'Mother brought it over.' She hastily defended her wearing of the dress.

A sudden gleam in Cole's eyes, quickly suppressed, betrayed his amusement at her predicament. Darn him! He was far too perceptive.

Charles and her mother looked around at the sound of her voice. 'Lindsey, you grow more beautiful every day,' Charles boomed.

'And you lie more every day,' retorted Lindsey.

'It's the dress,' said Caroline decisively. 'She made it, you know,' she added, turning to Cole. 'Such a saving when you can make your own clothes.'

'Mother!' Lindsey's insides knotted up. Was Caroline going to play matchmaker tonight of all nights? 'Cole isn't interested in my budget.'

Charles came to her rescue. 'Still think you ought to have a feather in your hair if you're going to wear an Apache dress,' he said, referring to an old joke.

'Apache dress?' Cole queried.

'Charles's idea of a joke.' Pointing to the peach, rust and turquoise bands that edged the cream-coloured sundress Lindsey explained, 'This trim is called Seminole patchwork.'

'Based on how the squaws applied their warpaint?' Cole asked drily.

'Hardly.' Lindsey ignored the implications of Cole's comment. 'In the eighteenth century the Seminole Indians of Florida used to trade with the Spanish settlers for fabric. The Indians thought the fabric was pretty colourless and they devised this technique to brighten it up.'

'You really are very talented,' said Cole quietly. Lindsey eyed him suspiciously at the compliment, but then decided that was Cole's way of apologising for ribbing her about wearing the dress when she had no choice.

Caroline broke the awkward silence. 'Darling, you are a marvel. Cole's house is wonderful. I'm ready to move in!'

'Charles might have something to say about that,' Cole teased. 'Meanwhile, why don't you have Lindsey show you the rest while I wash some of this paint off?'

As Cole left the room, Charles hastily offered to go and carry in the food from the car. Caroline laughed as he walked outside. 'He's afraid if he looks too interested I might decide to re-do our house.'

Lindsey grinned. 'I wouldn't have the nerve to put him through that misery again.'

'Men,' Caroline disparaged. 'They'd live in caves, if we'd let them. Although I have to admit that Cole was very brave turning you loose in here with all this navy blue paint. I wouldn't have had the nerve, but it looks fantastic.'

'I think he did have qualms, but he seems pleased with the results.'

'I do like Cole.' Caroline stole a glance at her daughter. 'He's such a fine young man, and so much fun to be around.'

'Watch out, or you'll have Charles getting jealous.'

'Charles likes Cole just as much as I do! Oh, I know you were just teasing.' She paused before adding thoughtfully, 'Sometimes Cole reminds me of your father. He has that same carefree air about him that characterised David, and, at the same time, he's every bit as sincere in his belief about the importance of what he does. Like Cole, David had a marvellous sense of humour, and just being around him made people feel better about themselves. But he wasn't content to just make them laugh. Your father was always the first to lend a helping hand, a strong back or a shoulder to cry on. I guess that's why it seemed so wrong when he died, because we need people like David down here.'

'I remember that we laughed a lot,' Lindsey said softly, not wanting to intrude on her mother's memories.

'I'm glad that you were old enough when he died so that you can remember him.'

'Do you still miss him?'

'Not all the time, not with the huge ache of loneliness that was there at first. No woman really knows how her husband's death will affect her until it happens. It was like a bomb had blown my life to smithereens, leaving behind an enormous crater that seemed bottomless. But time does heal all wounds, at least in my case. The sands of time, as they say, gradually filled that hole. There was you, my salvation,' Caroline smiled warmly at Lindsey, 'and then, of course, later there were Charles and Billy. I haven't forgotten your father, of course not. Something will happen and I'll think, I must tell David about that, he'll be so amused, and it will come over me that never again can I tell him anything.'

Lindsey could feel her eyes misting over at her mother's words. 'I'm glad you married Charles,' she said fiercely.

'Yes, Charles was good for both of us,' agreed Caroline. 'I've been lucky. Two wonderful husbands and two great kids.'

'There were times when I thought maybe it would have been better if you'd never met Daddy,' Lindsey said hesitantly.

'Oh no, darling, don't ever think that!'

'But don't you see? You're happy with Charles. If you'd met him first, then you would never have had to suffer.'

'And where would you be? Up cavorting with the angels still. No, Lindsey,' her mother spoke positively, 'marrying your father is one thing about my life I wouldn't have changed even if I could. Yes, his death was tragic, and it ripped my life apart. But that's the other side of the coin. David and I had so many wonderful times together, built up so many memories. Even had I known that we would only have nine years together, I still would have married him. When love flies by, you have to reach out and grab it with both hands. You can't expect promises that you'll be happy all the rest of your life. What do the kids say today? You have to go for it.' She gave an embarrassed laugh. 'I'm sorry, I didn't mean to get so carried away. You were going to show me the rest of Cole's house.'

Impulsively Lindsey hugged her mother. 'Thanks for telling me. I don't think I ever really understood before.' Looking down, she studied the rug at her feet for a minute. 'And I think I know what you were trying to tell me, but . . .' Unable to finish, she turned away to stare out of the window. Obviously Caroline suspected what had come between her and Cole, and thought that Lindsey was foolish to give up the man she loved because of her fears. Surely her mother's past lent weight to her opinion. Lindsey would think about it later.

'I just want you to be happy,' said Caroline softly. 'Now, how about this house tour?'

They ended up in the kitchen where Charles was putting a dish in the oven.

'Now, in here,' Lindsey pointed out, 'with the dark wood cabinets, we decided a lighter colour would be better.'

'She means she decided,' Cole interjected from the doorway. Bare feet and damp hair were evidence of his hasty shower. 'Lindsey made all the decisions. I just paid the bills.'

'A man's lot in life, my boy,' intoned Charles.

'The yellow does look good in here, don't you think, Mother? It sets off Cole's blue and white china.' Lindsey ignored the interchange between the men.

'You know it does. The whole house is marvellous.'

Well, it still needs a few touches. A few plants in strategic places, and maybe a stained glass window in the living room—a shop down on Tejon has a perfect one. Can't you just picture the sun shining through the coloured glass on to the sofa?'

'Maybe you'd better start moonlighting, Cole. Believe me, once a woman decides to re-do a house, there's no end to it,' Charles said with a teasing look towards Lindsey.

'You mean I may have started something that I can't stop?' asked Cole in mock horror.

'Precisely.'

'Oh, pooh,' Caroline retorted inelegantly. 'Be nice or you won't get any dinner, Charles Jeffries. And it's your favourite casserole.'

It was later, over dessert, that Caroline had her idea. 'Cole, you ought to have a house-warming.'

'It's a thought,' he admitted as he forked in a large piece of apple pie.

'Seriously,' Caroline insisted. 'You said you wanted to get married. Well, here's this gorgeous house that any woman would love and . . .'

'Really, Mother, Cole doesn't need a house to persuade someone to marry him!' interrupted Lindsey indignantly. The odd silence that followed her remark reminded her, too late, that she herself had rejected Cole.

Cole chose to ignore Lindsey's statement. 'The more I think about it, the more I like your idea of a party, Caroline. I'm not sure that I know much about what giving a big party like this calls for. Would you be willing to help me out?'

'Lindsey . . .' began Caroline.

'No way,' he interrupted with brutal honesty. 'Your daughter may be a whiz with a paintbrush, but she's disaster personified in the kitchen. Not that I want you to have to do any cooking,' he hastened to add. 'Just help me plan and I'll do the cooking.'

'You?'

'Cole's grandparents had a café down in Texas, Mother. I admit he's right when he implies he can cook rings around me,' said Lindsey.

'Not much of an accomplishment,' he teased.

'That's gratitude for all the work I've done here,' Lindsey pouted at him.

'When this house nets me a bride, I'll let you be in the wedding,' promised Cole.

'Never mind that,' she snapped. 'Just hurry up and find a wife, so I can quit wasting so much of my time on your house.'

'Lindsey!' Caroline was appalled at her daughter's rudeness.

'Don't worry about it, Caroline,' Cole said. 'Lindsey is just tired. She's worked pretty hard all weekend.'

'If I'm so tired, I'd better go home,' said Lindsey sharply, standing up from the table. Cole's patronising tone was more than she could handle. The way he kept talking about about his future plans in front of her, you'd think he'd forgotten that only three months ago he'd claimed he wanted that future to include her. It was more than she could bear. Besides, Cole was right. She was tired, bone-weary. Funny how she hadn't noticed it earlier during dinner.

Driving home, she thought back to her conversation with her mother. Caroline had said that her husband's death had ripped her life apart, leaving behind an enormous void. Lindsey knew exactly how her mother had felt. Ever since she had rejected Cole, she'd felt like the walking wounded, and Cole wasn't even dead. In fact, he was very much alive.

Very much alive, and obviously not suffering nearly as much as she was from their ill-fated love affair. He was even planning a party to find a wife—a wife who wouldn't object to what he did for a living.

Not that she cared. Just because she didn't want to marry Cole it didn't mean that he should remain a bachelor the rest of his life. If he chose such a dumb way to get a wife, it was of no concern to Lindsey. So what if she had decorated his home? Obviously, having done her part, she was no longer necessary to him. She wasn't about to cry any crocodile tears if she wasn't invited to his party. She wasn't the least bit interested.

And she certainly wasn't going to ask Cole anything about it, she told herself as she drove out to his house late in the afternoon. Her only reason for going was to deliver his towels and sheets. While she could have called him to collect them, she wanted to see how they looked in place. Seeing Cole again would be strictly coincidental.

Cole had company. Lindsey didn't recognise the second car parked in his drive, and momentarily she contemplated driving away without stopping. That would be pretty silly considering her errand would only take a minute. She was still arguing with herself when Cole answered the door.

'Lindsey! What a surprise!' He grabbed some of the packages which were slipping from her arms. 'What's all this stuff?'

'Your sheets and towels. You told me to buy you some new ones,' she reminded him breathlessly.

'So I did.' He ushered her inside. 'You remember Cheryl Davis?'

Wine glass in hand, the trim brunette looked thoroughly at ease curled up on Cole's sofa. 'Hi.' She lifted her glass in cool salutation, the knowledge clearly written on her face that she'd supplanted Lindsey.

'If I'm interrupting anything——' said Lindsey stiffly.

'No problem. How about a glass of wine?' A twitching muscle in Cole's cheek told Lindsey more than words that he was amused at the situation.

She stiffened at his easy assumption that she was jealous. 'Thank you. I'll just go and put these on first.' She smiled vaguely in the general direction of the sofa before turning towards the bedroom.

'I'll help.' Cole was close behind her.

'Are you and Cheryl working on a project together?' Lindsey asked casually.

Cole grinned. 'You could say that.'

Meaning no, she thought huffily. Grabbing a corner of the sheet, she ripped it from the bed.

Cole eyed her thoughtfully. 'Angry about something?'

'No. What would I be angry about?'

He shrugged. 'I thought maybe you were annoyed to find Cheryl here.'

'Who you spend your time with is no concern of mine.'

'Exactly.' Cole spoke with soft, deadly emphasis.

Lindsey paused, a pillow clutched to her stomach. 'Meaning?'

'Meaning, I know how hot-headed you can be at times, and I just want to make sure that you intend to behave yourself.'

Giving the pillow a quick snap in its case, Lindsey threw it down on the bed. 'Are you afraid I might embarrass you?'

Cole gave a low, amused laugh. 'On the contrary. I'm afraid that you might embarrass yourself.'

Lindsey stalked into the bathroom. 'Rest assured,' she said coldly, 'I'm not the least interested in your new girl-friend.'

'Good.' He leaned nonchalantly against the doorjamb watching her put away his new towels. 'I like them,' he said approvingly.

'Let's just hope your girl-friend likes them.'

'Do I only get one?' Laughter lurked behind Cole's watchful eyes.

'Even you can only handle one at a time!' she snapped, considerably ruffled by his teasing.

He reached out a lazy arm and gathered her close to his chest. 'Did I ever thank you for all your work on the house?' he asked, his warm breath eddying against her cheek.

'No—yes—I don't know,' stammered Lindsey, her heart rioting at his touch. She put her hands on his chest to push him away, but somehow they kept moving until they met behind his neck. A firm hand propelled her chin upward and he lowered his head until her mouth was only inches from his. She closed her eyes to block out the intent look on his face. Sensing the nearness of his lips, her own quivered softly in anticipation. A light kiss was pressed in the corner of her mouth, the pressure deepening until her lips parted to welcome his intimate exploration. The sensations Cole was evoking travelled down her body and she pressed closer to his firm, muscled bulk. She felt his body tense, and then his hand encircled her neck, a rough thumb caressing the pulse beating wildly at the base of her throat. The simple gesture sent the blood coursing through her veins, and she could feel her breasts swell with desire, the tips taut with longing. Seeking relief, she brushed against his chest. As if he sensed her need, Cole captured the throbbing globes in his large palms, the heat searing her skin through her clothing.

The voice calling plaintively from the living room brought her to her senses. Cole's arms released her, and she stepped back. She felt a small whisper of satisfaction as she glimpsed the flicker of frustration that crossed his face.

Cheryl called again. 'Do you two need any help in there?'

Cole shook his head ruefully, a whimsical smile twisting the corner of his mouth. 'For such a small package, you pack a pretty lethal charge!'

Lindsey straightened her clothing, unwilling to let Cole know how much his kisses had affected her. 'A simple thank you would have been sufficient,' she said coolly.

Cole laughed out loud. 'But not nearly as much fun!'

She stepped into the bedroom, just as Cheryl appeared in the doorway from the hall. 'I thought you might need some help in here.'

'I'm sorry we were so long,' Cole said smoothly. 'I was admiring the new sheets.'

Cheryl looked sceptical, but she refrained from comment.

'I really have to go,' said Lindsey hastily, wondering if her hair looked as tousled as her emotions felt.

A few minutes later, Cole's parting remarks echoing in her ears, Lindsey drove away. 'A shame you can't stay,' he had said, edging her out of the door. Obviously he could hardly wait to get rid of her so that he and Cheryl could become a cosy twosome. Perhaps he would finish with Cheryl what he'd started with Lindsey. She pushed such a hateful thought from her mind.

One thing was certain: Cole didn't need to give a party to find available women. He appeared to have all he could handle in Cheryl. It had been a silly idea of her mother's, anyway. No doubt Cole had rejected the idea that other night after she'd left. Careful questioning of her mother torpedoed that idea, however, since Caroline readily admitted that she and Cole were going full speed ahead with the party. Pressed for details, she slipped away from the subject, to Lindsey's deep annoyance. You'd think that Caroline could remember whose mother she was. Just because Cole was attractive and oozing with charm it didn't mean that Caroline had to forget her other responsibilites. Surely she had better things to do? Charles was probably pretty annoyed with his wife's activities.

She said much the same thing to Charles the next day when he came into the shop to ask Lindsey for some suggestions for her mother's upcoming birthday.

Charles just laughed. 'Caroline is having a wonderful time helping Cole out with his party. I just try to keep out of her way.'

'Surely you must have some idea what they're planning,' she said in exasperation.

'No, and I'm not going to ask,' he maintained. 'If I show any curiosity at all, the next thing I'll know, your mother will have me involved up to my neck. I know that she's having the time of her life planning this party, and that's all I need to know.' He frowned over at Lindsey. 'On the other hand, you don't look as if you're having the time of your life. Anything I can help you with?'

'What do you mean?' she parried.

Charles chuckled. 'Billy used to have that same look on his face when he had a problem, but was trying to make me think everything was okay.'

Lindsey smiled ruefully. 'Lawyers! You think you know everything!'

'And maybe you don't want to discuss it with me,' he said shrewdly.

Lindsey thought she detected a small amount of hurt behind Charles's words. 'I know I don't tell you this very often, Charles,' she began awkwardly, 'but I want you to know that I . . . I never regretted the day that Mother married you.'

'Thank you, Lindsey. You know, neither did I. In spite of what all the old fogies said.' He smiled in remembrance.

'What old fogies?' Lindsey's curiosity was aroused.

'You must be aware that your mom is quite a bit younger than me.' At her nod, he continued, 'Many of my friends, and even my partner, warned me against marrying her. "Charles," they said, "she'll still be a young woman when you're an old man. She'll want to dance and you'll want to take naps." And then, of course, worst of all, there was you.' He grinned wickedly across the counter.

'Me?' queried Lindsey.

'Sure. Here I was, to all intents and purposes, a staid old bachelor. I had Billy, but he was practically a man by then. People said if I had to get married, to marry a woman without children. They kept reminding me how an eight-year-old would disrupt my life. Well, they were correct in what they said.'

'Charles!'

'Honey, you did disrupt my life—and I loved it. Marrying your mom was the best gamble I ever made.'

'You mean you were worried that it wouldn't work out?' Lindsey asked in surprise.

'Marriage is always a gamble, honey, even when you think everything is in your favour. My first wife Eleanor and I had what everyone thought was a story-book marriage. Only it turned out we wanted totally different things, and she left me for another man. The only good thing to come from our marriage was Billy. Luckily Eleanor's second husband preferred to gloss over the fact that she'd been married before, and he didn't want Billy around to remind him. After they married, they moved to Washington, D.C., and we rarely saw Eleanor after that. If Billy was hurt by his mother's defection, he hid it well. He seemed more relieved than anything else. Eleanor wasn't the kind of mother who appreciated having a boisterous kid around.'

'I'm sorry that you and Billy had such a rough time of it.'

'We got over it.' Charles brushed aside her pity. 'But the point is, no matter how compatible a couple seems, there is no guarantee. Marriage is hard work, and predicting who will stay the course—well,' he shrugged, 'it just ain't possible.'

After Charles left, Lindsey tried to concentrate on her work at the shop, but his words kept intruding. He was as bad as her mother. They both thought Cole was so wonderful. Why couldn't they try harder to see her point of view? She wasn't asking for guarantees of happiness; she wasn't that stupid. Neither was she stupid enough to walk head first into a marriage that entailed as much risk as marrying Cole would. Couldn't they see that she loved him too much to bear losing him? Her mother said that she never regretted marrying Lindsey's father, that their moments of happiness outweighed the misery that followed. Lindsey thought back on the pleasant hours she'd shared with Cole. She had been so happy then. If only she'd been granted the ability to look into the future and foresee how unhappy she would be today.

She tried to shake herself free from the mantle of misery that covered her. Calling up friends, she proposed dinner, the theatre, picnics, anything to keep her busy and stop her from thinking about Cole and the fact that having used her to decorate his house, he had totally forgotten her. And that always brought her thoughts back to his latest crime. His proposed party irritated her like a burr under the saddle. She forced herself not to think about it. So what if she hadn't been invited? She didn't want to go anyway.

She only called Cole to ask if he wanted to look at a stained glass window. He picked her up at the appointed time, bought the window she suggested and even took her out to dinner, all the while maintaining an entertaining flow of conversation, much as if she were his maiden aunt, she thought in disgust. Not once did he allude to his house-warming party. Lindsey went home and threw her prized pillows across the room.

Houseplants were her next reason for calling him.

Once again he arrived on time, approved her selections and made arrangements for the plants's delivery. With a show of great concern for taking up her time he refused her offer to come out and place the plants. He did, however, treat her to dinner and a movie. She had no idea what they saw. At the door he kissed her goodnight so thoroughly that she was tingling clear down to her toes when he left. He didn't invite her to any party. Lindsey kicked her dining room table so hard it was a wonder nothing broke.

She was wandering aimlessly about the stock room at the store the next day when Ann called to her that someone was there to see her. Sure that her visitor was Cole, Lindsey hurried from the back room. The sight of the man standing there waiting for her brought her to an abrupt halt. 'Ross!' she exclaimed.

'Hi, Lindsey. I finished early at court and I thought I'd wander over and see if you'd like to take in a movie tonight.'

'Thanks, Ross, but not tonight.' Had he forgotten that she'd told him she didn't want to go out with him any more?

'You don't still have that bee in your bonnet about us not dating any more, do you?' he asked loudly. 'You know I'm crazy about you.'

Out of the corner of her eye Lindsey could see Ann and her customer pretending not to listen. Lindsey sighed. Trust Ross to pick a public place to make his declaration! 'Could you lower your voice?' she hissed. 'We discussed all this last week, and I told you then I thought it would be better if we didn't date any more.'

'Better for whom?' he asked plaintively. 'Not better for me. I don't want to think that we're all through.'

'Ross, get it through your head. Not only are we all

through, we never even got started.' Intent on convincing him, Lindsey paid no attention to the bell announcing another customer coming through the door.

'Hi. Not interrupting anything, am I?'

The thread of amusement in Cole's voice immediately told Lindsey that he had overheard her remark and had quickly grasped the situation. 'There's nothing to interrupt,' she answered coldly.

Cole narrowed his eyes thoughtfully at the hostility in her voice, before turning to Ross. 'My name is Cole Farrell. You must be Ross Waverly.' He extended his hand.

'How do you do.' Ross took the extended hand and shook it briefly, as if the touch of Cole's hand were distasteful.

Ignoring the obvious implication that his presence was intrusive, Cole spoke effusively. 'I'm glad to meet you at last. I've heard a lot about you.'

'From Lindsey?' asked Ross, almost in spite of himself.

A gleam of laughter lit Cole's eyes. 'No, from Charles and Caroline.'

'Oh.'

Almost as if he hadn't heard the woebegone monosyllable, Cole continued smoothly. 'Now that I've met you, I hope you won't mind if I ask you a favour.'

'What?' Ross asked warily.

Lindsey had the curious feeling that Cole was maintaining his calm demeanour at considerable cost. Hints of suppressed amusement deepened the laugh lines around his eyes, but his voice was serious enough when he answered Ross. 'I'm giving a house-warming party this weekend, with Caroline's help, and I'd appreciate if if you could escort Lindsey.'

'Certainly, I'll be happy to,' said Ross, ignoring Lindsey's protest. 'I'm surprised that you're not picking her up yourself.'

'Hosting duties, you know how it is,' Cole said airily in a man-to-man tone of voice.

'Oh sure,' Ross agreed.

'Good. That's a load off my mind. I didn't want Lindsey driving back and forth alone on the interstate that late at night.'

'I could go with my parents,' said Lindsay, provoked by Cole's officious behaviour.

Cole turned his back to her. 'Listen, it's been great meeting you, Ross. Looking forward to seeing you again. Lindsey can give you all the party details later. Now I know you'll excuse us. I need to discuss some decorating details with Lindsey.' One hand on Ross's shoulder, Cole had the other man out of the door before Ross realised what was happening.

'I am not going to your party with Ross,' Lindsey said in biting tones as Cole turned back to her.

'Well, Ross can probably find another date,' Cole said with comfortable conviction. 'I'm sorry that you won't be there, though. I was looking forward to introducing my decorator to everyone.'

'Are you implying that if I don't come with Ross, I'm not welcome at your party?' asked Lindsey heatedly.

'Certainly not. It's just that I wouldn't want your driving out there alone on my conscience.'

'If it worries you so much, I'll come with Caroline and Charles.'

Cole shook his head. 'They plan to come out early and help me set up. I wouldn't think of allowing you to do that, not when you've done so much already.'

'Then I'll get myself another date,' she snapped.

'Sorry, that would ruin my guest list. Guess I'll just have to have my party without you.'

'You are saying I can't come without Ross!'

He headed towards the door, calling back over his shoulder. 'I'll give Ross a call and tell him when the party is.' 'Don't bother! I'm not coming.'

Giving her an airy wave, Cole disappeared out of the door.

# CHAPTER SEVEN

LINDSEY was still fuming over Cole's arbitrary disposal of her person three days later while she waited for Ross to pick her up to go to the party. It was gradually borne in on her that Cole was serious: if she didn't come with Ross, she wasn't welcome. She tried to convince herself that she didn't want to go to his stupid party, but she knew that wild horses couldn't keep her away. She had contemplated going alone, but was well aware that Cole was all too capable of somehow putting a spoke in her wheel if she tried it. She was surprised that he hadn't called to check if she were following his orders, but she supposed that Caroline had probably kept him informed. Her mother was building up a long list of things for which she would have to answer to Lindsey.

Ross had taken her acceptance for granted, an assumption that provoked Lindsey no end. He was like a limpet, thanks to Cole. What right did that man have to interfere in her life? His petty idea of revenge for how she'd acted in front of that woman, no doubt. She wondered if Cole was still dating her—not that Cole's love affairs were of any interest to her. Going to the party tonight, she might be able to discover whom Cole was pursuing, but that was entirely incidental. Her main reason to go was that she was proud of how Cole's house had turned out. Why shouldn't she go and take the credit for the job?

She had finished dressing too early and now had to wait for Ross. Nervously she checked her image in the mirror. Perhaps a little more eye make-up. There wasn't much she could do with her hair, but it didn't look too bad. Surely the large golden hoops at her ears gave her a sophisticated air? She smoothed silky fabric over jutting breasts. Every night this past week had been spent creating the tomato red outfit, and the end result gave her immense satisfaction. Harem pants and a short-cropped bare camisole were both trimmed in trapunto edging. She'd quilted the matching jacket to lend strength to the light-weight silk, and a Chinese-inspired crane and lotus blossom design emblazoned the back. The jacket, of course, would be removed when she got to Cole's, allowing her to exhibit large expanses of lightly-tanned skin. She frowned. Maybe the top was too plain. A quick rummage in her jewellery box turned up just what she needed: Billy had bought her the thin gold chain in south-east Asia, and the delicate Oriental charm that hung from it slid between her breasts. Cocking her head to one side, she studied the final effect and decided it would have to do. It wasn't as if she were setting out to impress anyone.

At the pealing of the doorbell she hastily gathered up her bag and jacket. Ross said little on the drive out to Cole's house, which was fine with Lindsey, engrossed in her own thoughts as she was. It was ridiculous to be so nervous about a silly old party, but there was no denying the mixture of relief and apprehension that she felt when they at last pulled into Cole's driveway. The drive and entrance were bathed in light, while music spilled from the brightly lit house. Through the windows could be seen a large group of people milling about. Lindsey spotted Charles dispensing drinks in the kitchen.

Cole met them at the door, and taking Lindsey's hand he drew them into the house. 'Welcome to my humble abode. Not really so humble after Lindsey finished with it.' He spoke over her head to Ross. 'She's as talented as she is beautiful—and tonight that's very beautiful indeed.' His warm gaze approved her appearance, sending a warm glow to Lindsey's middle.

'Yes, Lindsey is quite the little home-maker,' Ross agreed with a patronising air.

'Obviously you've never cooked for him!' Cole spoke softly into Lindsey's ear, amusement coating his low voice.

Lindsey opened her mouth to dispute his disparaging assessment, only to be rendered speechless by a disturbing light in Cole's eyes. Dumbly she shook her head in speechless agreement. A look of satisfaction passed so fleetingly over Cole's face that Lindsey wondered if she'd imagined it when he moved her and Ross quickly along while he greeted the buxom blonde who entered behind them.

Too buxom, too blonde, and her aquamarine dress made her look fat, Lindsey decided with malicious enjoyment. Even the sight of Ross eyeing the blonde in lusty appreciation of her very visible charms failed to disturb Lindsey, suddenly secure in the knowledge of her own satisfactory appearance this evening. 'Do you want to find Mother and Charles to say hello or would you prefer to stand here and ogle?' she asked drily.

'I wasn't ogling,' he denied stiffly. 'I thought maybe I knew her from somewhere. She looks familiar.'

Lindsey barely listened to Ross's explanation. Maybe Cole's party was the answer to at least one of her problems, anyway. Looking around, she certainly could see a number of what appeared to be unattached, attractive women. Perhaps Ross's interest could be guided in other directions. She would gently call his attention to some of them. 'Cole certainly seems to have invited more than his share of beautiful women here tonight. I wonder where he found them all. That even looks like Ann over in the corner.' At her astonished stare, the tall brunette waved and moved in her direction. It was Ann.

'Hi, Ross. Hi, Lindsey.'

'I didn't expect to see you here tonight.'

Ann lifted an eyebrow at Lindsey's stiff tone. 'Cole invited all of us at the shop. He was in one day when you weren't there.' As Ross strolled off to greet Charles, Ann added anxiously, 'Does that upset you?'

'No,' Lindsey snapped. 'Why should it upset me?'

Ann shrugged. 'I wouldn't want you to think we were poaching or anything.'

'Certainly not. Cole means nothing to me.'

'That's what we were led to believe, but I wondered just now . . .' Ann's voice trailed off.

'Led to believe by whom?' asked Lindsey suspiciously.

'Cole. He said that the party was his opening salvo in a wife-hunting campaign. We all thought he was probably kidding, but at the same time . . .'

'At the same time, you're available,' Lindsey drily finished the other woman's thought.

'And interested,' Ann said as she strolled away, leaving a furious Lindsey in her wake.

Just why she was furious she wasn't sure. Cole had said all along that he would start looking for a wife as soon as the house was done. It wasn't his fault that she really hadn't believed him—but a person didn't just set out to get married. The whole idea was crazy. What did she care anyway? It was Cole's business, not hers.

'I don't own a house, but my apartment walls are sadly in need of paint.' The deep, teasing voice at Lindsey's side jerked her from her bitter reflections and, turning, she saw that she was being appraised from head to toe by a tall man who forcibly reminded her of someone else. She frowned in an effort to remember.

'Did I say something I shouldn't have?' the man asked, with a whimsical twist of his lips.

Lindsey smiled. 'It's just that you remind me of someone. I can't think who—I know! Kelly O'Brien.' She produced the name triumphantly.

Brown eyes lit up. 'Good old Kelly. My room-mate at the zoo.'

'At the zoo?' she asked in bewilderment.

'The Academy.' He brushed aside her question. 'Where do you know Kelly from?'

Explaining that Kelly was in her brother's squadron in Germany led to the telling of the circumstances surrounding their meeting. In retrospect, the misunderstanding seemed more amusing than it had at the time.

At any rate, her audience howled with laughter. 'If that isn't just like Kelly. Incidentally, I'm Terry Sullivan—yes, another mad Irishman,' he conceded at the look on her face. 'And you're . . .?' His voice lifted on a note of enquiry.

'Lindsey Keegan.'

'Well, Lindsey Keegan, I'm very glad to meet you. The woman over there who credited you with the remarkable transformation of Cole's house neglected to add your name.'

Lindsey looked in the direction Terry indicated and saw Caroline wink at her. Swallowing a giggle, she said, 'That woman is my mother.'

'I should have known. She's as beautiful as you are.'

Making it clear that he considered that he had won the door prize at the party, Terry had no intention of giving it up. With Lindsey's arm tucked into his, they made the rounds, Terry introducing her when it appeared that he knew many more of the guests than she did. He was an amusing partner, and his evident admiration went to Lindsey's head like champagne. A couple of times she caught Cole frowning in their direction, an action which spurred her on to laugh louder and cling harder to Terry's arm.

Lindsey was breathless from dancing to a fast tempo when Cole came over to her and Terry. The two men greeted each other with the ease of long friendship, although Terry raised an enquiring eyebrow when Cole draped his arm casually over Lindsey's shoulder. 'You don't mind if I borrow my decorator for a few minutes, do you? She's needed to settle a point about the kitchen.'

Terry readily acquiesced and turned back to some of his other friends. Lindsey knew that while he found her attractive, he was in search of nothing more than an entertaining companion for the evening. An attitude that was a relief to her, as she had no intention of adding any more entanglements to her life at present. 'What's the problem in the kitchen?' she asked, more to make conversation than because she was really interested. Cole's inexorable hand in the small of her back propelling her out of the room made her somewhat nervous.

'Nothing.'

'Nothing? I thought you said . . .'

'I want to show you something.' Ignoring her protests, Cole guided her toward the door leading out to the garden.

Pine trees rose as stately sentinels against the navy sky, their black ragged tips reaching up to touch the intense golden ball which hovered just out of their reach. 'A full moon,' breathed Lindsey. 'All it needs is a wicked witch on her broomstick riding across the face of it.'

'You're a romantic soul,' Cole teased. 'I thought it looked more like a lovers' moon.'

'Then you should be out here with Cheryl,' she pointed out lightly, denying the pain her own words gave her.

'Is that a hint you want me to go and get Ross for you?'

'No, don't bother him,' said Lindsey hastily. 'He . . . he's . . . that is . . . it would probably take you for ever to find him and it's too chilly to stand out here waiting.' She shivered to enforce her statement.

'You should have told me you were cold,' he chided. 'I tend to forget how these Colorado nights cool off. And you're not exactly dressed for the Arctic north. Here.' He put his arms around her and pulled her in close to his chest. 'Is that better?'

Resisting the urge to melt back against his firm male bulk, Lindsey nodded in silent assent. Unspoken thoughts, unvoiced words, seemed to swirl about her. She could sense the tension in the air, a tension based on their past as well as their present. It threatened to overwhelm her, and, fighting off an overpoweringly sweet urge to surrender to the magic of the moonlight, she said abruptly, 'Your party is a great success.'

A burst of raucous laughter from inside gave credence to her remark. Someone had turned up the stereo and the heavy beat throbbed and hung in the night air.

'Yes, your mom did a wonderful job. She ended up doing most of the cooking, too.'

'I meant more than the food,' said Lindsey drily. 'I've never seen so many single women in one room.'

'I did have a little luck there,' Cole said modestly.

'Luck? It looks like you advertised in the paper! Single available male having party. You all come.'

He laughed. 'I just spread the word around work, and then Caroline helped, too.'

'My mother helped get you women for your party?'

'Sure, didn't you recognise Charles's secretary? And she brought a few friends . . .' His voice trailed smugly off.

'You ought to be standing out here with one of them,' Lindsey said stiffly. 'Perhaps Cheryl . . .'

'And you ought to be with Ross. Then maybe we wouldn't be letting this perfect moon go to waste.'

'What do you mean?' Lindsey asked rashly.

'Just this.' Cole turned her to face him, one arm holding her tightly bound while the other tipped her face up to his. 'If I were your lover, I'd want to do this . . . and this . . . and this.' His words were punctuated by tiny kisses on her forehead, nose, until finally, his lips settled lightly on her mouth.

Rocked by the wave of intense feeling that coursed through her body at the touch of his lips, Lindsey could only cling helplessly to his arms. She'd stop him in a minute.

But Cole was directing this play, and he pulled away before she was ready. 'Of course, a lover wouldn't stop there,' he whispered huskily.

'No?' Blindly following his lead, she was incapable of rational thought.

'No.'

She closed her eyes to blot out the feral gleam in his as he lowered his head. She could feel his breath in warm soft bursts as he whispered against her neck, 'Your lover would be tempted beyond endurance by your smooth shoulders and vulnerable neck, your perfume would go to his head until he didn't know what he was doing.' Bold fingers pushed loose straps over her shoulders. Lips followed where fingers had been. She swallowed, the movement attracting his attention, and he pressed his mouth warmly to the pulse which beat wildly at her throat.

The scent of his aftershave whirled around them, seeming to Lindsey to bind them in invisible ropes. When his lips returned to hers, she tasted the tang of wine which clung to them. A slight breeze had arisen and the rustling of the pines mimicked her restless thoughts and emotions. Cole's warm mouth abandoned hers, and she felt chilled in the night air only to feel fire licking at her veins as his warm lips trailed kisses down her neck to her shoulders. His breath came in harsh pants. She welcomed the cooling balm as he bathed her heated skin with his moist tongue. But such relief was shortlived, as nimble fingers unbuttoned the front of her camisole. Breasts, marble white in the moonlight, were exposed to the night's chill for only a second before being warmly encompassed by Cole's large, possessive hands. The tingling in her stomach surfaced to centre beneath his palms. She moaned in longing, a sound that was effectively stopped by Cole's mouth covering hers, only this time he arrogantly demanded that she open her lips to his thrusting tongue. There was no question of denial. The moon had bewitched her; she had no will of her own. Drifting away on the wings of Cole's lovemaking, the party inside, their unsolvable differences, all of these faded away.

Cole's withdrawal brought her back to reality. Standing back from her, he buttoned her dress, as if he knew her fingers were incapable of operating at that point. Her skin was still electrified from his touch, and she trembled when his knuckles brushed the valley between her breasts. She dared not speak for fear her voice would betray the depths of her emotions.

'Ross must be wondering where you are.'

The casually spoken words were a blow to Lindsey's already tattered emotions. He had been playing with her, taunting her with the knowledge that his embrace could produce such a flaming response. He must hate her to treat her so spitefully. Steel flowed back into her spine, and she faced him defiantly. 'Why did you do that?' she demanded.

'Kiss you, you mean?' He shrugged. 'Why not? A full moon, a beautiful woman who's willing . . .'

She flinched at the word willing, but she couldn't deny it. She'd made no move to discourage him; she never did—a fact he was quick to take advantage of. 'Revenge?' she asked dully. 'Is that what this is all about? You just can't forgive the fact that I brought you to your knees in front of your friends and then left you without a backward glance, can you?'

Her outburst only amused him. 'Surely you can't say without a backward glance? Do you seriously expect me to believe you've never had a moment of regret for walking out on me in Germany?'

'Believe what you want,' she spat. 'You will, anyway.' She turned to walk away.

Firm hands held her shoulders immobile. 'Poor Lindsey.' Cole's voice was unexpectedly gentle. 'You don't know which way is up, do you?' Not waiting for an answer, he pushed her towards the house.

The hostile beat of the music that blared from within underscored Lindsey's anger and confusion. She was as upset with herself as with Cole. Having made her decision about him, why couldn't she let him go? She didn't have to melt into his arms at the slightest invitation.

Cole's arm barred her from opening the sliding door that led back into the house. 'Are you all right?'

'Of course,' she answered stiffly. 'I'm tired. I think I'll see if Ross is ready to leave.'

'Speaking of Ross,' Cole paused. 'He was watching you earlier flirting with Terry.'

'I wasn't flirting,' she denied wearily. 'We were merely enjoying each other's company. Terry is a fun person to be with.'

'I hope you can convince Ross of that. He didn't seem very happy when you two were dancing. Ross seems a nice guy, I'd hate to see him get hurt.'

'That's great, coming from you!' she retorted. 'You didn't seem to be so worried about what Ross might think a few minutes ago.'

'That's different. Ross already knows that you rejected me. He's not concerned about me.'

'And how, may I ask, does Ross know about you and me?'

'I told him.' Overriding her spluttering attempts to interrupt, he went on, 'I thought he might be worried about all the time we were spending together getting the house ready, so I explained that you were looking for someone with a more conservative life style, like his. Remembering him from the airport, I figured he's the type who needs a little shove in the right direction.'

'You have no business interfering in my life like that!' Lindsey cried indignantly.

'C'mon, I felt sorry for the guy. You pick him up and drop him like an old shoe.'

'I do not!'

'If you weren't interested in him, you wouldn't have asked him to bring you here tonight.'

'I didn't ask him,' she denied furiously. 'You did!'

'Did I?'

'You know very well you did.'

'I guess it slipped my mind. That just goes to prove that I always have your welfare in mind,' he said virtuously. 'I certainly didn't want you to feel lonely tonight.'

'I would have done just fine without your help, thank you. As you pointed out earlier, Terry Sullivan was certainly taking pains to keep me entertained.'

'You wouldn't be interested in him.'

'That's all you know, Cole Farrell. I'm very interested in him. Once he told me he'd got out of the Air Force, then I knew I was going to like him very much.'

'Are you?' Cole opened the sliding door and ushered her inside. 'Then I guess Terry didn't get around to telling you what he does now. He flies for the airlines.' With that parting shot, Cole left her standing by the door as he answered the summons of a brassy blonde.

When Ross found her only minutes later, Lindsey was still raging over Cole's audacious behaviour and hurtful remarks. Her sense of ill-usage was not lessened when Ross immediately began to interrogate her about her absence. 'What's it to you where I've been?' she asked furiously.

Taken aback by her anger, Ross stammered, 'Well, I thought—that is . . .'

'Whatever you thought, you thought wrong. I keep telling you that you and I are nothing more than friends, and I don't allow my friends to dictate my actions.'

'But . . . but Cole said . . .'

'And don't tell me what Cole said! I have no desire to hear about his warmed-over advice.' Over Ross's shoulder she could see Cole standing by the buffet being fed titbits by a tall, slender brunette. Cheryl Davis. She remembered that she had told Cole that she was tired. 'I want to go home,' she told Ross.

In spite of her protests, Ross insisted on going over to thank Cole for inviting him to the party. Knowing that Cole would place the correct interpretation on her refusal to do the same, Lindsey went with Ross, inwardly seething at his untimely sense of social etiquette.

Forced to wait while Cole chatted with a voluptuous redhead, Lindsey grew even more irritated. Did these women have to fawn all over him? When the context of the conversation taking place before her pierced her own dark thoughts, she was forced to bite her lip to forestall angry comment.

'Cole, honey, why did you paint the living room this awful dark colour?'

'Don't you like it?' Dancing lights showed all too clearly Cole's amusement as he looked at Lindsey over auburn curls.

'This whole room seems so cold and bare to me.' The redhead shivered artistically, causing her chest to quiver impressively.

'What would you suggest I do to improve it?' Cole's look told Lindsey he was deliberately egging the woman on, enjoying Lindsey's growing outrage at this disparagement of her skills.

'First of all I'd put in wall-to-wall carpeting. It's easier to take care of,' she added prosaically. 'Ruffled curtains at the windows would cosy the place up, too.' Carried away by her own enthusiasm, the woman failed to note either the gathering storm clouds on Lindsey's face or the discomfort on Ross's. Cole was clearly amused.

Breaking in on the conversation before Cole led the redhead to say something even more outrageous, Lindsey snapped, 'We're leaving now.'

'Must you?' he asked politely, his eyes riveted to the

redhead's amply-displayed cleavage.

Making a sound perilously close to a snort, she pivoted on her heel, and, grabbing a reluctant Ross, who was also bemused by the redhead's charms, headed towards the door. Behind her back she heard the redhead plaintively asking Cole who she was.

'Lindsey? She decorated the place for me.'

'Oh, no!' the redhead squealed, before succumbing to a fit of giggles.


Recurring images from the party the preceding night kept ruining Lindsey's concentration as she worked on a commissioned silk pillow the next day. It was a welcome relief when the phone rang—until she discovered who was on the other end.

'Just wanted to tell you how impressed everyone was last night with my new place.' Cole's deep tones came over the wire.

'Especially your redheaded friend,' said Lindsey involuntarily.

'Come on, Lindsey. You didn't take her criticism seriously, did you.'

'You led her on just to get my goat!' she cried, recalling Cole's amusement the evening before.

He laughed. 'You can't expect her to have good taste on top of her other multiple charms and talents,' he said provocatively.

'That's a chauvinistic remark if I ever heard one! Besides,' she added primly, 'I wouldn't know about her talents.'

'Surely it's obvious?'

'Did you call me just to discuss your friend's charms?'

'It always seems to me the best part of a party is talking about it after it's over. By the way, speaking of charms,

Terry Sullivan was smitten by yours. I told him he was wasting his time.'

'Would you get your fingers out of my social life? I can do just fine without your interference. First Ross, and now . . .'

'Oh, I see what it is. Ross made a pest out of himself last night, did he? I suppose he saw us out on the patio.'

'Ross did not make a pest out of himself last night,' Lindsey cried. 'No thanks to you.'

'Hey, don't blame ol' Ross's devotion on me. He was hanging around you long before I came on the scene. You aren't forgetting that touching airport scene, are you?'

'How could I? You keep ramming it down my throat!' When he failed to comment, she added, 'If you only called to harass me, I'm busy.'

'Don't you want to hear about my progress?'

'No. What progress?' Lindsey twisted the phone cord uneasily.

'Thanks to your great work on the house, I have several ladies who are dying to move in. Did you notice the blonde?' Not waiting for Lindsey's answer, Cole continued, 'Would you believe she's a home economics major?'

'No.'

'That was a rhetorical question,' he chided. 'She is, and she's coming out to cook me dinner tonight. Beef Burgundy, Rice Pilaf and Black Forest Gâteau for dessert.'

'How nice,' said Lindsey weakly. Judging by Cole's enthusiasm, the old adage about the way to a man's heart being through his stomach was true. 'How does Cheryl feel about that?'

'Don't know. She left early this morning for Alaska.

I'll ask her when she gets back if you seriously want to know.'

'Never mind,' she said hastily.

Cole laughed. 'It's been nice chatting with you, but I need to do a little shovelling out from the party before Marilou comes over.' He hesitated. 'I don't suppose you . . .'

'No!' Lindsey exploded. The nerve! Asking her to come and help him clean house before his date got there. Slamming the telephone down on its base did little to relieve her indignation.

Tossing aside the pillow, she decided to call her mother. Caroline's chatter would take her mind off other things.

'Darling, can I call you back tomorrow? The Martins are over, and we're playing bridge.' Her mother's preoccupation sounded clearly over the phone. 'It wasn't anything important, was it?'

Just that my life is a shambles, Lindsey muttered to herself as she hung up. For the millionth time she cursed the bad luck that had sat her next to Cole on the plane. Not bad luck, she reminded herself; her own fears were the sole cause of her present misery. Sitting home thinking about Cole in the arms of other women, she could feel the jealousy eating away inside her.

When she was a little girl, she had believed in stories that ended with happy ever after. Then her father died. Not that her life had been totally miserable after that. There had been awful times, but then Charles and Billy had become part of their lives. She had meant it when she'd told Charles she was glad he had married her mother. Charles had given Caroline her second chance at happiness. Chances were, somewhere out in the world there was a man for Lindsey, a man who could make her forget Cole and the unhappiness she'd suffered because of their break-up. Just as Charles had brought Caroline out of her mourning, maybe some man could bring her out of hers.

What was she saying? One couldn't compare Caroline's and her situation. Caroline's love had died; Cole was vibrantly alive. The key to Lindsey's happiness or misery lay in her own hands, not in the hands of fate. Restlessly she roamed through her apartment. Helen, Charles, Caroline—each had tried to point out to her that no one knew what tomorrow would bring. Their voices echoed in her head. He's in more danger on the highways, Helen had pointed out. No guarantees, said Charles. And last, her mother's words. When love flies by, you have to grab it.

Other memories came to mind. Her father's accident. How frightened she'd been on the plane. Cole's understanding and willingness to help her fight her fears. The dreadful, agonising ordeal of waiting to hear if Cole lived or died. She had chosen a safe future over one promising uncertainty along with happiness, but her chosen path had only led to misery. Could it be that she was wrong and everyone else was right?

Lindsey picked up the pillow she'd been working on, but gave up after a few stitches, viciously jabbing the needle into the fabric. She was so confused; she didn't know what she thought any more. If only there were some way to show everyone how she felt, to lay out her thoughts and feelings so that she could weigh what was important to her, to help her decide what to do.

The half-finished pillow lay in her lap, silently rebuking her idle hands. Impossible to work, yet she had so many commissions awaiting her attention. This pillow, plus several others, an evening coat, two wall hangings, and, of course, the quilt for the General.

Almost immediately an idea came to her. A fibre artist, her medium was cloth, not words. She'd make a quilt. Feverishly she searched among her supplies for the materials that she needed. Boxes were flung helter-skelter, packages ripped open, and sketches hastily made as the ideas flowed non-stop. It was almost dawn before she dropped wearily into bed.

The next day was someone else's turn at the shop, but Lindsey was up early and back in the extra bedroom that served as her workshop. She had decided that she would do as much appliqué and quilting by machine as possible in order to complete the quilt that much faster. Her fingers flew and the machine hummed. When the phone rang she was surprised to see that it was after five in the afternoon. She couldn't remember eating breakfast or lunch.

Cole was on the other end of the line. She didn't tell him about the quilt. Not that she had an opportunity; he did all the talking. She stuck her tongue out at the phone as he described his delicious dinner of the night before. When he went on to tell of his plans with the redhead for that evening, she was wetting a thread with her tongue and only grunted. Cole seemed to think the sound was one of encouragement and went on in great detail. Lindsey was so absorbed in her project she barely listened to him, and was relieved when he at last hung up.

That set the pattern for the next week. The other women at the shop understood how a project could be all-consuming of one's physical and mental efforts, and they made no objection to covering Lindsey's days at the shop. Used to her ways, her mother laughingly told her to give her a call when she surfaced. Phone calls from Cole were the only interruptions that dragged her from her workroom, and although she listened daily to his descriptions of his dates, such was her preoccupation with the quilt that his conversation and their relationship seemed to be of another time and place.

She did hear when he said that he was going to be out of town for a few days. His parents were celebrating their wedding anniversary. Lindsey volunteered to water his plants, and he told her where he'd hide a key. She redoubled her efforts, determined to finish the quilt before he came back.

Jabbing the needle into a pincushion, Lindsey dropped the heavy mass of fabric on her lap and stretched. Tense muscles creaked as she worked the kinks out of her neck and shoulders. There. The quilt was done, and Cole wasn't due back until tomorrow. She couldn't wait. Rolling it up, she grabbed up her car keys and bag and headed out of the door.

At Cole's house she watered his plants before spreading the quilt on his waterbed. Before her lay the entire catalogue of her feelings. Now Cole would understand. Lindsey felt an enormous sense of relief. The pressure of the past week was lifted, and all she wanted to do was catch up on her missing hours of sleep. Stretching sore and tired muscles, she let herself out of his house.

The drive to Cole's house the next day seemed endless. What a fool she'd been! She had come back from Germany in mourning. Her behaviour had been exactly the same as her mother's following the death of her father. She'd lost weight, tried to use work as an anodyne for pain, cried herself to sleep night after night, and why? She was causing herself the very pain which she said she couldn't bear. The difference was, Cole wasn't dead. He was vibrantly alive, alive and wanting to share that life with her. Her heart was buoyant, her mind calmed by her decision. She was eager to share her thoughts and resolution with Cole.

In spite of the flashing lights and numerous police cars, Lindsey was so engrossed in her thoughts that she didn't notice the accident until she was almost upon it. Even then, her entire attention was concentrated inward on the coming encounter with Cole and she paid no attention to the activity beside the road as she inched by following the patrolman's signals. It wasn't until she was safely past that she caught sight of one of the vehicles involved in the massive crash. A small red sports car lay forlornly to one side, a wheel still spinning aimlessly in the air, the top smashed beyond repair. A giant fear clutched at her heart. No! Not now! Unconsciously her foot pressed down harder on the accelerator.

The car's tyres screamed in protest as she sped around the corner into Cole's driveway. In the act of taking his suitcase from his car, Cole looked up in surprise. Lindsey slammed down on her brake pedal, bringing the car to an abrupt and screeching halt. Jumping from the car, she threw herself into Cole's astonished arms.

'Thank God!' she sobbed. 'When I saw the accident, I thought it was you!'

Cole's arms tightened around her, offering immense comfort. 'The accident on the interstate?'

Lindsey nodded. 'When I saw the red car . . .' A sob tore from her throat, and she shuddered at the memory of the crushed car.

'It's all right, honey. Everything's okay, don't cry. I saw the accident, too. What in the world made you think I was involved?' He tilted her chin up.

She lowered her lashes to blot out the disturbing light in his eyes. 'The car looked like yours.'

'Lindsey, Lindsey.' Cole shook his head in loving

exasperation. 'My car is a Porsche. The car in the accident was a Datsun 240-Z.' He wiped the tears streaming down her face.

She sniffed. 'It was red,' she said defensively.

'That's true,' he said sombrely, but the glint in his eye gave him away.

'It's not funny! You might have been . . . been . . .' She blew her nose with the handkerchief he handed her.

Cole retrieved his suitcase from where it lay in the dust. 'Come on inside so I can change out of my travel clothes. I think we need to have a little talk.'

Suddenly shy, Lindsey refused to meet his eyes as she preceded him into the cool confines of his house. Declining his offer of a drink, she drifted into the living room. Cole grabbed a beer from the refrigerator and then went towards his bedroom, tugging at his tie.

Seconds later he erupted from the room, a look of fury on his face. Yanking Lindsey up from the sofa by her arm, he ruthlessly propelled her into the bedroom. 'If this is your idea of a joke, I don't think it's very funny!' he said savagely.

Caught in the middle of blowing her nose, Lindsey could only stare helplessly in the direction of Cole's stabbing finger.

At first glance the sky-blue quilt appeared to be a record of man's flight. In the centre was Daedalus, high above turbulent blue seas, his white-feathered wings outspread, the sun beating down on man's first attempt to fly. It wasn't until one looked more closely at the appliquéd picture that the body of Icarus, Daedalus's son, could be seen, half floating on the waves, his melted wings flotsam upon the water. Randomly dispersed, tiny vignettes embroidered in black surrounded the central scene. Here was a plane plummeting towards land, over there flames and a mushrooming cloud of black smoke. One scene showed children playing with their fathers while a small girl stood alone off to one side. A close-up of a woman's face showed large tears marring her beauty, while a black-clad widow held a folded flag. Unopened parachutes plummeted from the skies, and planes collided in mid-air. Rows of white crosses marched across the foot of the quilt while black zigzags of lightning flashed across the top.

Cole shoved her in the direction of his bed. It didn't take a genius to realise that he was livid with rage. 'I think you've made your point. Is that why you rushed out here to welcome me home? So you could see my reaction to that piece of trash? Well, you've seen it, and now you can take it and get out!' he exploded.

Lindsey reeled under the lash of his furious words. 'You . . . you don't . . . don't understand,' she faltered. 'I was . . . was trying to . . . to explain . . .'

'I understand perfectly,' Cole bit off the words. 'You don't have enough guts to marry me, but I refused to have a safe little affair with you. You thought you were safe when you ran away in Germany, but then I followed you here, and you realised that I wasn't going to let you get away from me this time. Knowing that your own desires were weakening the wall you'd put up between us, you decided that this—this abomination would make me so mad that I wouldn't have any more to do with you. Too weak to make your own decisions and stick with them, you wanted me to take the decision-making process out of your hands. Well, I will, lady: I want you to get out of my life and stay out!'

Lindsey shook her head, half laughing and half crying. Cole had just admitted that he still wanted her. 'I can't get out. I promised you a quilt, and since you obviously don't like that one, I owe you another one.'

'You owe me nothing,' he said bitterly. 'Take that—that thing and get out!'

Suddenly Lindsey was mad. Did Cole really think that she would have gone to all that work out of meanness? She turned on him, a small, angry whirlwind of sound and fury, her outstretched finger jabbing him in the chest. 'Fine—I will get out. I don't want anything to do with a man who thinks he knows everything!' She grabbed the quilt, and, rolling it into a bulky bundle, thrust it under her arm. 'Go on back to Cheryl Davis and all your redheads and blondes whose IQs are probably the same as their chest measurements!' Furiously she marched to the front door, stopping long enough for one parting shot. 'If you marry someone who puts in beige wall-to-wall carpeting, I'll never speak to you again!' The door slammed decisively behind her.

Halfway home the irony of the situation hit her. How could she have let Cole goad her into walking out like that? Billy was right, she thought ruefully; sometimes the red in her hair did come through. She had to go back and explain to Cole. Never in a million years would she have expected him to jump rashly to such an erroneous conclusion.

At her apartment she exchanged one quilt for another. The phone beckoned, but what if Cole hung up on her? She would go back to his house, and this time he'd listen to her if she had to hogtie him first. His car was still in the drive when she got there, erasing the fear that he wouldn't be home.

She didn't wait for Cole to come to the door but walked right in. He was out on the deck staring off into the distance. The sound of her heels clicking on the floor alerted him to her presence, and he whirled. Lindsey almost lost her nerve then at the savage expression on his face, but her steps quickened and she was in the bedroom before he was through the sliding glass doors. Flinging the quilt on the bed, she was smoothing it out when Cole came through the bedroom door in a rush. At the sight of the quilt he came to an abrupt halt. The silken squares of greens, blues and oranges shimmered in the half light of the setting sun.

'What's this?' he demanded harshly.

'The quilt for your bed.'

'Selling it to me because of a guilty conscience?' he jeered.

'I told you before—it's not for sale.'

'Don't tell me you're giving it to me?' Cole's face twisted with scorn.

'I won't. I couldn't bear to part with this quilt.'

'You just said it was my new quilt.'

'No, I didn't. I said it was the quilt for your bed.'

'I'm not in the mood for word games,' Cole said savagely.

'Then shut up and listen.' Lindsey slowly and carefully spaced out her next words. 'It's your bed, but it's my quilt.'

'Meaning?' Cole moved nearer, intimidating her with his implacable bulk.

She edged back until she was brought up short by the side of the bed. 'Meaning,' she cleared a lump from her throat, 'meaning, where the quilt goes, I go.'

A deadly silence met her announcement. Gathering the courage to look up into Cole's face, she shivered at the brooding expression in his eyes. Heartsick, she looked away. Cole wasn't interested any more. Rough fingers in her hair forced her to face him. 'Marriage?' he asked tersely.

'Marriage.'

'Damn you!' He shoved her on to the bed before dropping down beside her. Cradling her face between his large hands, he muttered, 'Do you know how close you came to getting your neck wrung?' His descending mouth cut off her answer.

Later she lay beside him, tucked up against his shoulder. 'Do you suppose you could explain that other quilt to me now?'

'I could have explained it earlier if you'd have given me half a chance,' Lindsey retorted. 'I never dreamed you'd go off half-cocked like that.'

'Normally I wouldn't, but I doubt that I've been normal since I met you,' he said, sarcasm coating his words. Leaning down, he nipped her on the shoulder. 'You have a lot to answer for, my love. Now, tell me about the quilt.'

'Ever since you walked away from me that day in Germany after I'd refused you, I've been horribly miserable,' she told him. 'I thought I would get over you, but then you showed up in Colorado. I hated you for not understanding my fears, for refusing to quit your way of life for me. It seemed that I couldn't make anyone understand how I felt about your flying. You, Mother, Charles—you all thought that I was foolish and craven to let my fears stand in the way when it was obvious to everyone how much I loved you. I was so frustrated, and so unhappy, and it was all your fault.'

Cole frowned down at her, but before he could say anything, she pressed a finger against his lips. 'Let me finish. Maybe it was jealousy, maybe the advice that Helen, Charles and Mother all tried to give me began to soak in, maybe I just grew up a little. All I know is that gradually I realised that what I was going through, missing you, longing to be in your arms, was little different from a widow mourning her lost love. But I was mourning a love I didn't have to lose. I agonised at the thought of you in someone else's arms, and all the time, the cure for my pain was right there in my own hands. All I had to do to stop the pain was to stop fighting love. Those thoughts were all so mixed up in my mind that I decided to make the quilt to explain to you how I felt, and at the same time, clear up the mess in my own head. I was driven to finish it, working night and day, and then something I didn't expect happened. Coming up with the ideas, trying to think of all the horrible things that could happen . . . I cried when I contemplated those sorts of things happening to you. Making the quilt acted as a catharsis for me. By the time I'd finished it I knew for certain that I wanted to marry you, to grab what life has to offer now. If something happens to you tomorrow, at least I'll have had today.'

Cole kissed the top of her head. 'You brought me the quilt to explain why you'd changed your mind, and I threw you out.'

'You were beastly.' Lindsey started to snuggle deeper in Cole's warm arms when a sudden thought struck her, and she quickly sat up. 'I changed my mind, but I never asked you if you changed yours. Maybe you don't want to marry me any more.'

Cole grabbed her hips and pulled her down to rest on his broad chest. 'I haven't changed my mind.'

Honesty forced her to add, 'I can't promise I won't drive you crazy worrying about you, and I still don't want ever to set foot on a plane, but I'll try and overcome my fears.' She hesitated. 'Maybe you were right that I should seek professional help. Do you have any idea what you're in for?' she asked, half laughing, half crying.

Cole hugged her tightly. 'I'm willing to take a chance if you are.' He tipped up her chin. 'I'll still have to go back to flying.'

'I know.'

'But not all the time. I'll do my best to make it easier for you.'

There were better ways to thank him than with words. Satisfied, Cole said, 'You never stood a chance. I've been planning to marry you all along.'

'What do you mean? You let me leave Germany.'

'Merely a strategic retreat to gather my forces,' he murmured as he planted a series of kisses along her chin. 'I knew where to find you, and I was counting on this assignment to get me here.'

'What about all that nonsense about buying a house and getting a wife?' Lindsey asked suspiciously.

'Helen's idea,' he said simply.

'Helen?' she gasped.

'I needed allies. She maintained you'd never be able to resist decorating the house.'

'What about Cheryl?'

'I told you that she and I were working on a project together. Can I help it if you didn't believe me? Cheryl has a boy-friend in Alaska, whom she's visiting right now.'

'What about your blondes and redheads?'

'Red herrings to keep you from running scared.'

'More than red herrings, all those dates,' said Lindsey scornfully.

Cole laughed, a low, amused sound that turned her bones to butter. 'There were no dates. I just told you that to have an excuse to call you every night. You got so interested in my pseudo-love-life that it never occurred to you that it was you I was talking to on the phone every day.'

'I wasn't that interested.'

'Admit it. You were jealous.' Laughter danced in his eyes.

'I was not.' Lindsey turned her head away.

'Liar.' Cole rolled over on the bed, imprisoning her with his body. 'Tell the truth.'

Lindsey felt her muscles quivering in response to his blatant masculinity. 'Maybe a little.' He bent his head, and breathlessly she asked, 'Why did you keeping shoving Ross at me?'

'To keep you busy. I knew he wasn't a threat to me, and I wasn't taking any chances on some other guy waltzing in and grabbing you right from under my nose.'

'Poor Ross. We both used him,' she said in a conscience-stricken voice.

Cole laughed. 'What do you mean, poor Ross? Didn't you hear him bragging about your home-making skills? We've saved him from a life of disillusionment. On the other hand,' he leered down at her, 'it's not your cooking skills that I'm interested in.'

Soft colour warmed Lindsey's face, and she could feel her pulse racing at the hungry look in Cole's eyes.

'It's not?' she asked breathlessly.

'No.' His mouth closed on hers. After a few moments of demonstrating what he was interested in, he nibbled his way to her ear. 'Lindsey?'

His warm breath sent desire rippling through her body. 'Hmm?'

'Don't bother to bring a nightgown on our honeymoon.'

'Why not?' Who could think with Cole's hands wandering in bold possession?

'I'll loan you a T-shirt.'

Her last thought before surrendering to the tidal wave of desire that promised to engulf her was that, no matter how many years together she and Cole were granted, they would be good years, filled with laughter and love.

# JULIE ELLIS

### author of the bestselling
### *Rich Is Best* rivals the likes of
### Judith Krantz and Belva Plain with

# THE ONLY SIN

It sweeps through the glamorous cities of Paris, London, New York and Hollywood. It captures life at the turn of the century and moves to the present day. *The Only Sin* is the triumphant story of Lilli Landau's rise to power, wealth and international fame in the sensational fast-paced world of cosmetics.

---

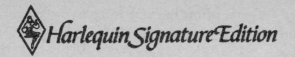

# Carole Mortimer

## *Merlyn's Magic*

She came to him from out of the storm and was drawn into
his yearning arms—the tempestuous night held a magic
all its own.

You've enjoyed Carole Mortimer's Harlequin Presents
stories, and her previous bestseller, *Gypsy*.

Now, don't miss her latest, most exciting bestseller,
*Merlyn's Magic*!

## IN JULY

All men wanted her,
but only one man would have her.

### Desert Storm
#### Nan Ryan

Her cruel father had intended
Angie to marry a sinister cattle baron twice her age.
No one expected that she would fall in love with his
handsome, pleasure-loving cowboy son.

Theirs was a love no desert storm would quench.

STM-1